Praise for the
Award Winning

THE ALIEN SKILL SERIES

Reviews:

"This book sings with hope and beats with adventure."

"I'm spellbound!"

"Loved the ending, it was so amazing and powerful!"

"Fast paced with epic scenes."

"A great environmental lesson for young adults."

BOOKS BY RAE KNIGHTLY

Prequel
The Great War of the Kins
www.raeknightly.com

THE ALIEN SKILL SERIES
Book 1
Ben Archer and the Cosmic Fall
www.amazon.com/dp/1989605192

Book 2
Ben Archer and the Alien Skill
www.amazon.com/dp/1989605095

Book 3
Ben Archer and the Moon Paradox
www.amazon.com/dp/1989605141

Book 4
Ben Archer and the World Beyond
www.amazon.com/dp/1989605044

Book 5
Ben Archer and the Star Rider
www.amazon.com/dp/B086RK31LT

BEN ARCHER

and
THE WORLD BEYOND

The Realm of the Sea

Rae Knightly

For information, go to:
www.raeknightly.com

Cover design by PINTADO
Book Formatting by Derek Murphy @Creativindie
Published by PoCo Publishers
ISBN Paperback: 978-1-989605-04-2

First Edition: April 2020

For our oceans.

CONTENTS

CHAPTER 1 *Motu Oné*

Ben Archer pressed his forehead against the window of the spaceship. The crystalline waters of French Polynesia stretched out before him. An uninhabited island curved out of the sea to his right, displaying its sugar-coated beaches, lush bushes and coconut palms.

The alien who sat at the controls by Ben's side brought the spacecraft to a gentle stop, letting it hover above the water without making a sound.

The size of a fighter jet with two sets of wings and just enough room to fit eight people in its hull, the black craft escaped radar detection with ease. Nevertheless, the thirteen-year-old squinted as he scanned the sparkling horizon, confirming that no humans sailed in the vicinity.

Cumbersome reports of UFO sightings could complicate their mission and were best avoided at this point.

Ben puffed his cheeks, the hot cabin making him sweaty under his diving suit.

Guess the Toreq forgot to install air conditioning...

"Mesmo, are we going or what?" he said, backing away from the spacious window and throwing an annoyed look at the humanoid. "Gotta save the world, remember?"

The coral reefs off Motu Oné, one of a string of islands in the remote South Pacific Ocean, had been on Ben's mind for weeks. Yet, now that he was here, at last, Ben had to admit he had gotten up on the wrong side of the bed. Ever since he'd said goodbye to his mother that Sunday morning, a dark cloud had followed him from his pillow to this idyllic place. Mulling over why that could be, he turned to look at Mesmo.

His alien friend didn't answer—too absorbed with his task as he shifted through holographic screens that floated before his face. The shadow of intricate symbols scrolled down the man's high cheekbones and honey-coloured eyes.

Irritated by Mesmo's silence, Ben sighed and crossed the hollow interior of the vessel to activate a switch. It released a metallic door that slid open, letting in a hot breeze that smelled of summer at the beach. He plopped down at the edge of the opening, swung his bare feet outside and dipped his toes into the transparent sea, admiring the pure white sand that lay ten feet below the surface. He reached for one of his fins and squeezed his eyes shut as he tried to pull it over his foot.

"Give me a moment," Mesmo said in a delayed response to Ben's question.

Ben knew he was reviewing the data given to him by one of the Wise Ones, who had last studied the area five years ago. "Jeez! You've gone over that ten times already," he said, grimacing as he struggled to put on the second fin. "Let's get our message out, Mesmo."

"You're right," Mesmo said, tearing his eyes away from the screens and leaning back in the pilot seat. He clapped his hands together. "Let's do this."

Ben watched him from the corner of his eye, becoming seriously offended with the uncooperative fin. "Mom's gonna need to dye your hair brown again," he said, noting that the roots of Mesmo's hair had turned white. Even though he looked like a normal man, the alien's otherwise bleach-white hair and unusual height could stick in people's minds.

"Yes, she told me." The alien tossed his flip-flops aside and removed his Hawaiian t-shirt, revealing his tanned torso. "So, are we going or what?" he poked, before taking three big strides across the egg-shaped interior and executing a perfect dive.

"Show off," Ben muttered, then whooped as his foot slipped into the stupid fin.

Mesmo resurfaced. He turned to face Ben and pointed behind him. "The coral reef's that way. Or we could try our luck farther out. There's a five thousand foot drop nearby—the entrance to the Pacific Ocean. Might be interesting..."

"No, thanks," Ben cut in, slipping his mask over his head and eyes. "I'm not trained for the deep yet. And besides, it would take me hours to decompress." He tapped his pressure gauge with his fingers.

"Come on, Benjamin, you don't need that old diving stuff. You know I can take both of us underwater." Mesmo's hands began to glow as he called up his inner power. The alien's fingers released a blue force that dented the surface of the sea until it reached Ben's feet. A large bubble surged from the water before the boy.

Trying to hide his admiration, Ben strapped

the air tank to his back. "Jeez', Mesmo. We've been over this. You know I have to do this on my own. It's not like you're going to be around every time I need your water skill. And this *old diving stuff*—as you say—is the best my backward little civilization has got for now, so deal with it."

"Suit yourself." Mesmo shrugged with a smile. His hands stopped glowing, and the bubble burst, splashing Ben.

"Ha-ha." Ben grimaced, before shoving the snorkel in his mouth and placing his hands at the edge of the door. But his right hand slipped on the wet surface, sending him tumbling out of the spaceship. The side of his head hit the water, shoving liquid into his mask. He tore at it, sending stinging salt water up his nose.

Spluttering and wiping at his face, Ben found Mesmo staring at him with one eyebrow raised. "Are you ok?"

Ben gagged at the sea-salt sliding down his throat. "Don't... you dare... laugh."

"I'm not," Mesmo said innocently, the corner of his mouth curling. "You know me. I'm incapable of humour."

"Yeah, right. But you sure learn fa..." Ben cut short because a familiar rushing sound filled his ears. He raised his hands, already expecting them to shine a clear blue. Ben closed his eyes and felt his own alien skill take over his human blood cells, the way it always did when an animal was nearby.

Trying to ignore his burning nose, Ben searched left and right. For the first time, he noticed how silent the ocean was. Wouldn't he be hearing a mingle of voices from sea creatures by now? He swam to the front of the spaceship and found the source that had activated his translation skill. A shiny black animal flopped around the surface. He reached out to it with his mind.

Hello? Are you in trouble?

Silence.

As he waded towards the creature through shallower water, Ben had to form a mental block to fend off fear that emanated from it.

Sh, it's ok. I'm here to help.

The animal twitched, and suddenly Ben recognized it.

A manta ray!

No bigger than a dinner plate, one of its triangular wings twisted in an awkward manner, deforming its sleek body. Leaning in closer, Ben understood the problem. The remains of a fishing net made from thin, nylon strings was wrapped around the young manta ray's body, pinning one of its wings over its back and hindering its movements.

Mesmo joined him, and they both set to work removing the entangled mesh. When they released the pectoral fin, the manta ray slid away in a hurry.

Ben and Mesmo exchanged a glance.

"It wouldn't even let me talk to it," Ben said, disappointed.

The alien placed a reassuring hand on his shoulder. "It's ok. We'll have better luck at the coral reef. They will listen to you there."

Ben tightened his grip on the nylon strings. "I hope so," he said. "Our lives depend on it."

CHAPTER 2 *Dark King*

After the manta ray incident, Ben and Mesmo dove under the sea and swam towards the area identified by one of the Wise Ones as a reef that teemed with life.

Ben was admiring the crystalline water and white sand beneath him when he noticed Mesmo waving him over to the edge of a rocky ledge located a few feet away.

Ben kicked with his fins, wondering what his friend had found. He stopped and grabbed on to Mesmo's arm in shock.

They stood at the edge of a mind-boggling precipice. The ocean wall dropped at their feet with no end in sight.

The boundary to the Pacific Ocean!

Ben's heart raced with a mixture of awe and excitement. He had only experienced this overwhelming feeling of being a speck of dust once before, and that had been in the depth of space. He glanced wide-eyed at Mesmo, who nudged his head to indicate they should head the other way.

Relieved, Ben followed the man away from the abyss and focused his attention on the outskirts of the atoll, where Mesmo had said the coral lay.

They found nothing.

Mesmo turned to Ben, his face slightly distorted by the air bubble that surrounded his head. He looked like a weird cosmonaut who had forgotten to put on his spacesuit over his floral swim trunks.

Bewildered, Ben pointed at the seafloor.

Where's the coral?

Mesmo understood his unspoken question and shook his head; *I don't know.*

They both frowned, then headed in different directions in search of the missing reef.

Ben swam over some broken pieces of shells and found a dead fish resting on top of the sand, but that was it. His stomach twisted with worry. Could the Wise One have miscalculated the coordinates?

Highly unlikely!

Besides, Mesmo had gone over the information in minute detail, to the point of irritating Ben.

He tuned in to his skill, listening for any signs of life. Finding none, he wanted to report to Mesmo but his friend was inspecting the sea bed some way off—too far to catch his attention. Reflecting on his dwindling options, yet reluctant to head back to the spaceship empty-handed, Ben's thoughts cut short when something moved out of the corner of his eye. He jerked around.

A few feet away, seaweed swayed above a lonely rock.

Chuckling nervously into his scuba snorkel, Ben gave himself a quick shake of the head, scolding himself for acting so jumpy.

S-s-s-s...

Ben froze.

Who's there? Show yourself!

His hands began to glow. Something lurked out there, alright. Breath quickening, he stared at the rock. Maybe the manta ray was stuck again?

Vowing not to succumb to fear, he kicked hard with his legs, hoping to reach the rock before the silent creature could take off on him.

Wait! I have to talk to you.

He stretched out his arm towards the hard surface of the rock, grabbed on to it and pushed himself around it.

Nothing.

He circled again, his hand brushing against the slimy seaweed, baffled at the absence of life. But then the seaweed floated down and clamped around his wrist.

S-s-s-s...

Ben's head snapped up.

That's not seaweed!

A tentacle curled up his arm, aided by a dozen reddish suckers.

"Mmm!" Ben yelled into his mouth-piece as a large octopus materialized through the algae.

A confusing mass of slimy arms coiled around his armpits and brushed across his face.

Before Ben could react, the creature clenched its grip and yanked him away from the rock. It headed to deeper waters, in the direction of the abyss with him in tow.

Ben looked on in horror. "Help!" he shouted, the word coming out as a useless mumble.

The octopus slid effortlessly over the sand, headed for the edge, and plunged over the precipice.

Ben's heart dropped like a stone with it.

Wait! Stop!

Speeding down the abyss, one sucker stuck to the side of his mask, Ben saw darkness becoming more oppressive, silence more crushing. He fought desperately with the octopus, but it only squeezed his arms more tightly.

Please! I came to help.

The octopus slowed, but not because of Ben's plea.

S-s-s-s...

S-s-s-s...

Ben's heart beat so loud he was sure it could be heard on the other end of the Pacific.

There's two of them!

The bulbous body of a second beast appeared in his field of vision, eyeing its struggling dinner. A multitude of arms coiled before him, sliding over his legs and body. They pushed him so hard, he hit the rocky wall and saw stars.

They're fighting... over me!

Ben couldn't figure out which way was up or down. His hands scraped the hard surface of the rock.

STOP IT!

His brain burst with angry words. This had

to stop!

The octopus's movements slowed. They spoke to each other.

What is-s th-this-s?

It s-speaks-s.

Ben felt their sense of curious caution. He jumped on the occasion.

My name is Benjamin Archer. Why won't you listen? I'm trying to speak to you!

He knew he was meant to say those introductory words, but his tone sounded harsh, fueled by a mixture of rage and panic that he couldn't suppress.

The fifteen-foot long creatures forgot about their scuffle. Their large, black eyes scanned him.

It wants-s to s-speak to us-s.

I'm taking it to my nes-st.

No! Its-s mine. I found it firs-st.

Tentacles reached for him again, gooey skin brushing his neck and arms. Ben's head swayed. The alien skill threatened to draw him into the beasts' minds because he could not control his fear.

The arms drew back slightly.

I don't like its-s s-skin. It is-s not good for eating.

The other octopus agreed. A similar thought

floated between the creatures. Ben caught a glimpse of it in his mind and shuddered.

Lets-s give it to the dark king.

Yes-s. A peac-ce offering.

To calm his-s hunger.

Yes-s. The dark king eats-s anyth-thing.

Even bad meats-s...

Ben's mind burst with anger and dread.

THAT'S ENOUGH!

He lashed the words at the octopus, who eyed him warily.

It became harder for Ben to think. How long had he been underwater? His air tank only allowed him an hour of swimming.

Listen to me. I came to give you a message.

The first octopus wasn't impressed.

Th-the dark king will dec-cide.

I'm not here for your dark king. I'm here to tell you something, and to find out what happened to the coral...

He stopped mid-sentence because both eight-armed mollusks moved aside briskly and clung to the abyss wall like spiders without letting him go. Ben's blood chilled as he heard them say:

He is-s already here.

Their rubbery bodies gave way to the ocean darkness. Ben blinked franticly, trying to make out the powerful beast that had entered into the outer vision of his mind. Whatever was out there caused his captors to show fear and reverence.

And then he saw it. The shadow of a great white shark streaked before him in the gloomy ocean.

CHAPTER 3 *The World Beyond*

Ben's sight blurred.

I can't be running out of oxygen now!

Even if he had been able to release his wrist from the octopus' grasp, he wasn't sure he wanted to know what his oxygen levels were. Not that it mattered. He was about to get mauled by a shark—unless the octopuses decided to cram him into their nest in some crevasse first.

Feeling lost without his sight, Ben went ahead and relied entirely on the information provided to him by his alien skill. He caught a clear feeling of mutual respect between the octopuses and the shark, and Ben realized that, although the latter was heavier and larger than the mollusks, the shark would have trouble taking on two full-grown octopuses if it had to.

The three creatures' attention turned to Ben, and, surprisingly, their feelings turned cold, as if they rejected him.

The eight-armed mollusks greeted the shark.

Dark king, we bring you a gif-ft.

The great white shark approached, its voice echoing in Ben's mind.

Why do you bring this creature from the world beyond? Of all living things, it is the one I trust the least.

Ben started. Was the shark talking about him?

The octopus spoke tentatively.

S-still, it is-s better than noth-thing, dark king.

Ben had had enough. He spoke with as much courage as he could muster.

I am Benjamin Archer. I will speak to you, and you will listen!

The shark's tail fin flicked in surprise. Ben felt the tentacles loosen just a bit around his arms. The cool sensations he had felt from the shark before, turned to interest. *You speak.* Black eyes watched him. *I have never met one of your kind who could speak the tongue of other living creatures. How can that be?*

Ben caught his breath. He had to act and fast.

It's a long story. There is no time to tell it now. I came to give you a message, and I came to check on the corals but found nothing. I want to know what happened, so that I can help.

The shark swam back and forth, considering his words.

Why do you lis-sten, dark king? This-s creature does-s not des-serve your attention. Take him, now.

Ben struggled against the octopuses' grasp, irritated by their interruption. He could not afford to lose the shark's attention.

The shark eyed him.

Why would you care about the corals? Your kind destroyed them. Your people raked the floor, broke everything. The fish have gone. Those who survived the attacks have starved to death. We are the only ones that remain, and our time is counted. How can you not know this, you, who come from the world beyond?

Ben caught the tone of accusation in the great beast's words. A wave of sadness washed over him. *I am sorry. This should never have happened. But that's exactly why I came. You see, I speak your language, and I also speak the language of my people. I wish to be the translator between our two worlds. I will be your spokesperson. Let me be your voice.*

While he sent out his thoughts, Ben tried to take small gasps of breath. He knew he was running dangerously low on oxygen. His brain fogged up, and his muscles numbed.

The shark showed interest in Ben's words, and the octopuses knew it.

Dark king. Do not lis-sten to th-this-s treacherous-s creature. It cannot be trus-sted.

Without warning, the shark lurched forward, snapping rows of razor-sharp teeth. Although it had only meant to startle the octopuses, it succeeded so well that they loosened their grip on Ben. His arms slipped between the tentacles.

Too shocked to react, Ben toppled down the chasm. He reached out, willing his arms and legs to swim, but instead, his right hand banged hard against the rocky wall.

"Ouch!" he mumbled, eyes watering. His foot hit a jutting rock. By some miracle, his left hand caught it as he tumbled past. He clung on for dear life.

BLOOD!

The shark's word boomed from the darkness.

I smell blood!

In a flash, the shark went berserk.

There was no escape.

Ben shielded his head with his arms and braced for the iron-clad jaws to close on him.

BANG!

Explosions blasted through the ocean.

Peeking through his arms, Ben watched a thick sheet of transparent ice barrel past him, separating him from the shark's attack.

The shark backed away, surprised, but not defeated. Already, it turned again. There was no talking to him now.

A slimy octopus tentacle wrapped itself around Ben's leg, tugging him off the rock.

SNAP!

A flash of lightning (or was it ice?) bolted through the water, slicing the tentacle from its host. Ben vaguely registered falling into a black spray of ink as the octopus scampered away. He rolled further down the abyss.

Then, out of nowhere, Mesmo caught him in his arms. The boy let himself go limp, though he remained conscious enough to know the shark lurked close.

The second octopus curled an arm around his wrist.

SNAP!

It, too, lost a tentacle.

More ink. More confusion. Frenzied jaws snapping at them from behind the artificial ice created by Mesmo's skill.

The alien sped up the chasm wall, carrying Ben.

Too fast.

Way too fast. "Mmm...mmm." Ben tried to warn his friend.

But Mesmo soared like a bullet towards clearer waters, oblivious to Ben's weak calls.

The boy's brain crushed under the pressure. He reeled as pain seared through his muscles.

As soon as they breached the surface, the alien man tore off Ben's mask and snorkel.

Thick liquid poured out of Ben's nose, turning the sea, red.

"Benjamin!" Mesmo's distraught call sounded distant.

Ben fought to control violent spasms that coursed through his body. "De-c-c-comp-p-p..." *Decompression*, he tried to say, casting a pleading look at his friend.

Mesmo held him tight. "I've got you," the alien said, his voice hollow with worry.

Darkness swallowed Ben.

I'm falling again!

"I've got you," the voice echoed.

* * *

Laura Archer rushed into the kitchen, emptied her half-empty cup of coffee in the sink, then buttoned up her suit jacket. She grabbed her smartphone out of her purse and checked for messages. There was nothing new since Mesmo's last text: RUNNING LATE. C U TONIGHT.

That was it. No further explanation.

She tapped her fingers on the counter, wondering what to do. If she delayed any longer, she'd be late for work. She checked the phone again and confirmed that the message had arrived in the early hours that same Monday morning. So, Ben and Mesmo would be home tonight.

Everything's ok, then, right?

Except that Ben was going to miss another day of school. She wasn't sure how she felt about that.

Ben's learning so much on his trips with Mesmo, she reminded herself. What school could offer those kinds of global field trips?

She wondered once more if she should have gone with them, but then stopped herself. She'd had enough adventures. Doing normal things helped her keep focused and anyway, at least one person in this household had to keep their two feet on the ground.

She only had herself to blame for worrying.

A loud knocking on the door startled her. She rushed to open it, wondering why Mesmo and Ben weren't coming home through the back.

Except it wasn't Ben or Mesmo. It was a young man with curly hair and a camera strung over his shoulder.

Laura blinked, raising her guard. "Yes?"

"Oh, hello, Miss. Sorry to bother you so early," the lanky man said, raising his sunglasses to rest on his head. "I'm kind of new to the area, and I guess I got lost. I'm looking for Joshua's Eco Farm. It's supposed to be the second exit after Chilliwack. Have you heard of it?"

Laura gave him a quizzical look. "Uh, no, sorry, I haven't heard of it. But this is the first exit, so you probably want to go back to the Highway and keep going till the next exit."

"Ah, ok, that would make sense," the man said. He backed away with a salute. "Appreciate it."

Laura nodded and inserted the key into the lock of the front door to leave for work, but the man just stood there.

"Say, Miss," he said. "Would this be the place

where *The Cosmic Fall* occurred?"

Laura froze with the key still in the lock. She took it out slowly and faced the man. "Why do you want to know?"

"I'm sorry. I should have presented myself," the man said, stepping forward and extending his hand. "I'm Jeremy Michaels, reporter with the Provincial Times."

Laura stared at his hand then shook it loosely, feeling goosebump rise on her arms. "A reporter?"

The man gave a little cough. "Yes, well, straight out of university, really. I'm on my first assignment."

He must have sensed her tense because he added quickly, "Oh, uh, not *The Cosmic Fall*. I mean, my assignment is to write an article on Chilliwack's organic produce. That's why I'm looking for Joshua's Eco Farm." He stared at the fields longingly. "But, yeah, coming here, I suddenly remembered *The Cosmic Fall* happened somewhere close, so I was wondering if you could point out the location to me."

"You won't find anything around here," Laura said. "You need to go into Chilliwack for that. The town hall can probably give you a lot more detail." She headed to her car. "Look, I'm sorry, but I'm late for work..."

The reporter caught on. "Of course! Of course!"

Laura slipped into the car seat and was going to shut her door when the reporter stepped forward and blocked it.

"So, like, you don't know anything about *The Fall*? I mean, from what I heard, the explosions woke up the whole town. You must have seen something," he insisted, infuriating Laura.

"Look, Mister Michaels, I wasn't living here at the time, ok?" she said, then pulled so hard at the door that he had to leap back, so it didn't hit him.

Laura glared at him as she turned the key in the ignition and sped away, watching the reporter stare after her in her rear-view mirror.

* * *

Soft, blurry light.

Ben's cheek stuck to a smooth surface.

The floor of the spaceship...

He recognized it because the metal wasn't cold and hard like iron but a softer version that copied his body's temperature. So why did he feel like a battered lump of clay trying to mould itself into shape again? Why did every extremity hurt?

Then he remembered the great white shark and gasped.

"Sh," Mesmo said beside him. "Lie still."

Ben's eyes focused. A soft blue glow travelled up and down his body, leaving him with a warm, tingling feeling. "Wha...?"

Mesmo sat cross-legged before him, forehead creased. "Relax. Give it some time," he said. The alien was biting his nails.

Ben had never seen Mesmo bite his nails before. *Mom does that, too.* "How long...?" he croaked.

"A couple more hours."

Ben tried to move his arm, but that only sent lightning-bolts of pain from his fingers to his shoulder. He sagged in resignation. *A couple more hours...* He scrunched his face, trying to ignore his screaming muscles.

"I don't get it," Mesmo said, interrupting the boy's inner battle.

Ben forced his eyes open a crack. "Wha'?"

"I don't get why humans have forgotten how to live under the ocean."

That was unexpected.

"Huh?"

"The A'hmun... you know, your ancestors? Well, if my people's history records are correct, the A'hmun built many cities under the vast oceans of their planet, Taranis."

Mesmo was trying to distract him from the pain, Ben realized. It worked. The truth was, Ben still hadn't quite wrapped his head around the fact that millennia ago, humans had originated from a distant planet called Taranis. Humans had called themselves *A'hmun* back then.

"Wha' happen' to Taranis?" Ben managed, welcoming Mesmo's diversion.

The alien shrugged. "Oh, from what I've heard, the planet has been uninhabitable for centuries, ever since the end of the Great War of the Kins." He looked down at Ben and added apologetically, "I guess my people didn't give it much of a chance of survival."

Ben felt a ripple course down his spine at the idea that an alien civilization had the power to wipe out life from an entire planet. Ok, maybe that wasn't exactly the kind of distraction he'd hoped for.

The A'hmun and the Toreq. A glorious past of ancient alien races, erased from human minds. They had been like brothers once. But then the War had broken out, leaving both civilizations in shambles. The Toreq had herded the few A'hmun survivors and banished them to a tiny, insignificant planet called Earth.

Earth isn't insignificant.

Ben clenched his jaw. He had admired his home planet first-hand from the cockpit of Mesmo's spaceship.

A speck of blue. A grain of sand lost in the darkness. Perhaps. But not for Ben. There was no darkness on Earth. It teemed with life, sounds, colours and emotions. Ben didn't care if the Toreq saw it as a mere prison for the remnants of their terrible enemies. He would protect and preserve it to his dying breath.

Ben exhaled slowly, clearing his mind and willing himself to be patient while he healed. He turned his head and watched the circle of light wash over him time and time again, soothing his aching body. He recognized the closed shaft. Mesmo's shapeshifting enemy—Bordock—had lain lifeless in this exact spot not so long ago. "What is this, anyway?" he said, unable to stop a shiver.

"Radiation," Mesmo answered. "It is removing the nitrogen bubbles from your bloodstream."

Radiation? Ben decided he didn't need any

more details, so he turned the other way and caught sight of thick, pink clouds outside the spaceship window. "Are we airborne?"

Mesmo nodded.

"How long have I been out?" Ben could feel his strength returning by the second.

"About ten hours."

"Ten hours?" He sat up this time, horrified, then shut his eyes as his brain exploded. "Ouch," he groaned, grabbing his head between his hands. He squinted at his friend. "Mom's going to kill us."

Mesmo lifted an eyebrow. "She can't do that. I just saved you."

Ben grimaced. He rubbed his throbbing head and admitted, "That didn't go quite as planned, did it?"

Mesmo jabbed his index finger at him. "Benjamin, you are diving with me next time."

CHAPTER 4 *Camping*

Ben stared out the window of the rowdy school bus and drifted into a daydream.

"...Matt Caine's in it too," a blond-haired boy commented from a row behind him.

"Yeah, he's the bad guy," a second teen agreed.

"It's showing tomorrow at 3.50, at the Star Theatre," a third one said, glued to his smartphone.

"Ok, great! So, who's coming?" The second one asked, to which all three cried "Me!"

"Hey, Ben, are you in?"

Ben turned, blinking. "Huh?"

"Dude! *Galaxy Hero* is on this weekend. Are you coming?" the blond-haired boy insisted.

Ben straightened. "Oh. Um, I can't. But thanks."

His classmate stared at him.

Ben cleared his throat. "Maybe next time. I promised my dad I'd help clear the yard."

The second boy groaned. "Again?"

"Didn't you do that last weekend?" the third one quizzed, pointing at Ben's bandaged hand.

The blond-headed boy shook his head knowingly. "Parents. They never give us a break..."

"I found the trailer!" the boy with the phone shouted.

"Lemme see!"

All three boys shoved into the same bus seat to peer at the small screen, freeing Ben from their attention. He turned and watched the passing scenery again, sighing inwardly.

The bus emptied a handful of students at a time until only Ben remained. Once on the outskirts of town, he said goodbye to the cheerful bus driver and began his walk up the dusty road towards the house his grandfather had left him and his mom.

His thoughts shifted to the three boys on the bus. In other circumstances, he wouldn't have minded getting to know them more. He would probably have fit in quite well, come to think of it, as he had noticed that they had timidly tried to include him in their conversations before. He'd also heard *Galaxy Hero* was a hit, and he knew without a doubt that the movie would be the talk of the class by next week.

He kicked at a stone, feeling guilty for thinking about a fictional movie, when, in the real world, he was stuck with major problems that required his full and undivided attention.

He straightened his backpack, then winced because he forgot he was using his injured hand. Although the gash he had obtained under the sea was healing nicely, it was a constant reminder of last weekend's failed outing.

Everything had gone wrong: the thriving coral reported by one of the Wise One had been destroyed, the creatures he had tried to communicate with had turned against him, and he hadn't even been able to deliver the carefully crafted message he and Mesmo had worked on.

And this hadn't only occurred in French Polynesia. Out of all the locations he and Mesmo had visited so far, only a few sustained a viable ecological environment to maintain animal life. And where animals thrived, a silent illness—caused by human contamination—infested them like cancer that risked declaring itself within a decade, a year, maybe even a month.

The future looked bleak.

If Mesmo and Ben didn't find a way to communicate with the animal kingdom, their future and that of humans was at stake. If humans didn't learn to live peacefully beside other living creatures and didn't help them with the healing process, there wasn't much hope of survival for any of them, human or animal. And, in the end, the wrath of the Toreq that hung above their heads like the sword of Damocles would come crashing down on them.

Ben's mood dropped a notch. He was failing grandly at his task. How was he ever going to bring everyone together?

* * *

Laura Archer cut a lemon in half with a sharp knife. "That pesky reporter was here again this morning. I spotted him from the window upstairs, taking pictures of the fields."

Mesmo lifted his head from the maps he was studying on the living room table. "He was?" He stood and sat by the kitchen island, where Ben's mother began to press the citrus juice into a jug of water.

Laura nodded. "High Inspector Hao called and said someone from the Provincial Times had left him a message. But he says said not to worry; he won't make a statement."

"Good." Mesmo nodded. "What else did our government agent have to say?"

"Nothing good," she said, grunting as a particularly hard fruit refused to release its juice. He took it from her, so she opened a drawer instead, picked out a large spoon and began mixing the fresh lemonade. "The government is hard of hearing. Preparing Earth for an alleged alien invasion is not exactly on their agenda." She picked up the knife again and rested her hands on the counter, thinking. "Only the highest levels of government have seen enough evidence to make them believe in the existence of the Toreq. James says not enough people are informed, meaning things will continue to move at a snail's speed. At this rate, two hundred years will never be enough to prepare a human defence against an alien attack."

Mesmo opened his mouth to speak, but she pointed the knife at him. "That said..." she pressed, "James continues to insist you do *not* reveal yourself to the world. At least, not yet."

Mesmo pressed his lips together. "Hm. You

know what I think about that."

Laura raised an eyebrow at him. "And you know what James thinks about that. You'd cause chaos and put yourself in danger. Give him some time to work on world leaders, to prepare them and pave the road. There's a right time for everything."

"You just said humans would never be ready to face my people. I still believe we need to speed things along. Give humans a nudge in the right direction. If I reveal myself as the extraterrestrial that humans have been searching for, we could at least start a worldwide conversation."

Laura dropped the knife on the counter, the metal clanking. Her face fell as she stared at him, then she admitted, "I don't think *I'm* ready for that..."

He placed his hand on top of hers. "I understand," he said. "But it is something we will need to discuss again in the near future. And it is also the reason I am meeting with the Wise Ones next month."

She gazed into Mesmo's honey-brown eyes. They acted like buoys she could cling to. The front door opened, so she put a finger to her lips. "Keep the reporter thing to yourself. I don't want Ben to worry."

She picked up the jug of lemonade and filled the three glasses, watching from the corner of her eye as Ben plunked his backpack on the couch and joined them by the counter. "Hi, honey, how was your day?" she asked, keeping her voice as light as possible, even though she noticed his tired eyes as she slid a glass his way.

"Fine," he answered glumly, gulping down the lemonade and glancing at the maps on the coffee table. "What's our next stop? Is it the Greenland ice sheet?" He questioned Mesmo with his eyes.

"Hey, hey, HEY," Laura called, waving her hands at them. "Guys, are you kidding me? There's no way Ben is going on another neck-breaking trip this soon."

"Oh, come on, Mom. We have no choice. There's too much ground to cover," Ben complained.

"Young man," she warned. "I forbid it. And besides, you're going to listen to me. Summer vacation starts in a week. I've set you up for a camping trip on Vancouver Island."

Ben set his glass down with a loud clunk. "*What?* Just like that? Without asking me?"

"There's no negotiating involved. You're going, and that's final. I want you to forget about your skill for a while. Go and have some fun, make friends, go hiking and swimming, eat marshmallows and tell ghost stories around a campfire. The world isn't going to change that much in a month."

"*A month?* You're sending me away for a whole month?" His eyes almost popped out of their sockets as he turned to Mesmo for help.

Mesmo said sternly. "I agree with your mother, Benjamin. She knows what's best for you."

"Oh, great! You're taking her side now!" Ben jumped off the counter stool. He glanced from one to the other. "I see, you're both in on it, aren't you? You want to get rid of me, just when there's so much to do, and so little time."

"Benjamin," Mesmo said gently. "I've seen you suffer from each of our trips. You carry a heavy burden, much too heavy for a human as young as you. It's affecting your mood and your sleep. It's all right to take a break. It will do you good. You'll come back strengthened."

"But we're meeting the Wise Ones next month! I thought..." Ben broke off, then shut his eyes and groaned. "You don't want me to meet them, do you?"

"I do," Mesmo insisted. "But not just yet."

Ben lifted his eyes and glared at him. "I thought we were in this together!" When neither Mesmo nor Laura moved, he yelled. "Fine! Just send me away then!"

Laura caught her breath as he turned and fled through the kitchen door. The hinges screeched as he stomped out into the back yard.

Mesmo jumped off the counter stool, but she held him back. "Leave him," she said. When he hesitated, she insisted, "He'll be fine. You know we have to send Ben away until that reporter stops snooping around, don't you?"

"But Ben hates us. Maybe this isn't a good idea after all."

Laura sought his eyes. "It is," she said, trying to sound strong. "Trust me."

Mesmo's shoulders relaxed, and he sat again. He puffed air out of his cheeks and nodded. "I trust you," he said.

CHAPTER 5 *Trespassing*

Jeremy Michaels parked his car on the lonely road next to the cornfields. He stepped out and swung his camera over his shoulder, breathing in the fresh air and taking in the lush hills that rolled down to the town of Chilliwack. Crickets chirped, birds swooped over the corn stems, and a soft breeze blew through Jeremy's curly hair. A bee buzzed by his cheek. He swiped it away with his hand.

He'd been here twice already: first, when he had asked that woman for directions a week ago, and again this morning. Then he'd spent all day at organic farms, but now, instead of heading back to the office, he'd found himself driving up the same dirt road for the third time.

What for? He didn't know yet.

Nothing of what he was seeing bore witness to the terrible event that had occurred here almost a year ago, when bus-sized meteors had plummeted from the sky and come crashing down in these very fields. It was as if *The Cosmic Fall* had never happened.

How strange!

Jeremy had at least expected some kind of commemorative plaque or government sign. He checked his smartphone again, making sure he had found the right spot, then scrolled over the articles related to the event, feeling stunned by the pictures of billowing smoke on the hillside, hovering army helicopters, worried locals...

Too bad I missed it.

He had spent last year's summer in New York, working on an internship to wrap up his Bachelor's Degree in Journalism. Yet, while the experience had been valuable, he had found himself butting against fierce competition from fellow graduates.

Had he stayed on the West Coast of Canada instead, he would have come rushing over to cover *The Cosmic Fall* and made a career breakthrough right there.

Sighing, he aimed his camera at the growing

crops and took some pictures, more out of habit than because he had noticed anything of interest.

A branch cracked. Whirling, he squinted into the gloomy forest to his left but saw nothing. His ears caught a strange sound, though, like some kind of motor running at low velocity.

Not a motor... Something else...

He stepped through the thick growth, trying to locate the origin of the humming. There was a weird blue glow in the trees alright, maybe the sun reflecting on something, and next to it, a cloud of black spots that moved so fast he couldn't tell what they were.

Leaves vibrating in the wind?

But there was no wind.

He took pictures with his camera, advancing with care. His shoe stepped on a twig. It snapped.

At once, the cloud of buzzing spots paused in mid-air. Then they charged at him, turning into a swarm of angry bees, and for a second, Jeremy saw chaotic darkness.

"Help!" he yelled, falling hard on his backside in shock.

Then, as quickly as they had come, the buzzing died down, and the bees disappeared.

Jeremy lay on his back, gasping. He checked his hands and touched his face, but didn't have a single bee sting on him.

"You know you're trespassing, right?"

Jeremy lifted his head in surprise and blinked at the teen who had just emerged from the trees. The boy looked about thirteen or fourteen, though Jeremy couldn't be sure because a light grey hoodie covered the boy's head, and his hands were plunged deep into the front pockets of his sweatshirt.

Removing a sharp twig that jolted into his back, Jeremy groaned as he got up on his elbows, then froze, because a black-and-white English Shepherd materialized from the bushes, lowered its ears and let out a barely audible growl. "Hey, control your dog, would you?" he said in alarm.

The boy stared at him, then nudged his head at the dog, who plopped down beside him and lolled its tongue.

"Just great," Jeremy muttered. He cast away the aggravating twig, then scanned the ground for his camera. He reached for the strap and pulled the camera up with him, checking it anxiously for scratches. Finding it intact, he let out a low breath of relief, then glanced around. "Did you see that?" he said, remembering why he had ended up on the ground in the first place.

The boy eyed him sharply. "See what?"

"Those bees!" Jeremy burst. "They swarmed me! Hundreds of them! I thought they'd turn me into meat skewers, for sure! But then they just flew off."

Leaving me with a sore backside.

The twenty-three-year-old wiped at the leaves and dirt stuck to his jeans and saw the boy shrug without answering.

Humph! Friendly townsfolk.

Jeremy swung the camera over his shoulder and frowned. "What's that you were saying about trespassing?"

The boy straightened with a slight air of defiance. "Well, you are. This is private property."

Jeremy snorted. "No, it's not. At least, not anymore."

A veil of doubt crossed over the boy's eyes.

Ha! Got you, there.

Feeling smug, Jeremy turned and headed through the brush, the boy and his dog tailing him. He broke into the fields and took in his surroundings, then pointed at an impressive mansion topping the hill to his right. "I did some research this week. This land used to belong to a wealthy businessman called Victor Hayward. But the government bought it from him recently. I figured they'd be wanting to turn it into some kind of national park or something, you know, so the public can come and learn about *The Cosmic Fall*, meteors and stuff..."

"How would you know that?" the boy demanded.

"Oh, right, *sorry*. Where are my *manners?*" Jeremy chided as he pulled his wallet from the pocket of his jeans and fished out a business card, which he handed to the boy.

The teen eyed it as if it were some kind of snake, then snatched the card and stuffed it into his pocket without even looking at it.

Jeremy lifted an eyebrow, then cleared his throat. "My name's Jeremy Michaels. I'm a reporter with the Provincial Times."

The boy took a small step back, though Jeremy couldn't tell if it was to balance himself or to put some distance between them.

The latter, probably.

He sighed inwardly. He was used to having people react like this when he told them he was a reporter. They either squealed with excitement at the prospect of being interviewed, or they backed away—either because they were shy, or because they had something to hide. "I came to write an article about the region's farms and their organic produce for the tourism section. But then I remembered that *The Cosmic Fall* occurred here, so I came to check it out." He paused. "You know about *The Cosmic Fall*, right?"

The boy wouldn't meet his eyes. "Sure. Who doesn't?"

Jeremy ground his teeth. "So, I guess you're trespassing, too, huh?" he poked. "I mean, aren't you a bit far from town to be on your own?"

The boy shrugged. "I live here." He gestured with his head in the direction of a large house, visible through a fringe of trees.

"Oh!" Jeremy's irritation evaporated like ice in the sun. He recognized the house. It was the one where he had stopped to get directions.

Show some professionalism, darn it—even if this is just a kid.

"So, you *do* know all about *The Cosmic Fall!* Do you know what it was like? I mean, it must have been terrifying!" He caught himself, realizing he was letting his emotions get the better of him.

The boy shrugged. "I wasn't living here at the time."

"Oh," Jeremy groaned, unable to hide his disappointment. That's what the woman had said, that she wasn't living here at the time. He gazed longingly at the house. "I wonder who was, then?"

To his surprise, the boy answered, "My

Grampa."

"Seriously? Do you think I could meet him?"

The teen avoided eye-contact. "You can't. He passed away last year."

"Shoot." The word left Jeremy's lips before he realized that this boy had recently lost close family. "Um, my condolences."

This week was becoming duller and duller. First, the boring organic veggie assignment, and now a missed opportunity to print a never-before-released interview with a possible direct witness of *The Cosmic Fall*.

But there weren't any witnesses—or were there?

He lingered on the thought. There were several houses in the area after all, yet he couldn't remember any mention of direct eyewitnesses to the meteor crash.

Weird...

Then there was the eerie glow he had gone to investigate in the forest behind him, just before the bees attacked him. It had to have been the sunlight, of course, but still...

"So, I'd better go now." The boy's words pulled Jeremy out of his thoughts. The teen had already retreated several steps, the dog never leaving his side.

"Oh, hey," Jeremy called after him. "What's your name, anyway?"

"Ben," the kid said, then turned and ran off.

Jeremy put his hands on his hips.

Ben... Just Ben. So now what?

Then it dawned on him that people around here were probably tired of shooing away curious onlookers who came to search for left-over meteor scraps. That would explain the woman and the kid's blunt attitude, for sure.

CHAPTER 6 *Tofino*

Ben watched the waves hit the hull of the ferry as it coursed across the Strait of Georgia. He did this for over an hour, sulking. Mountainous Vancouver Island stretched on the horizon under a blue sky scattered with clouds.

The island contrasted drastically to the little tropical bump that was Motu Oné, as this one was similar in size to Taiwan. Not only was Vancouver Island vast, but most of it remained empty of inhabitants. Covered in dark green Sitka spruce and snow-capped mountains, only a handful of towns and cities—Victoria and Nanaimo being the biggest of them—sprinkled the coastline.

Yet Ben wasn't heading to any of these. Once the ferry docked, he'd take a bus westward across the island to the Pacific side. There, he'd join a camping group in a town called Tofino, the population which had a grand total of two thousand.

Ben kicked the side of the railing in annoyance.

Could Mom have sent me anywhere more remote?

He sighed heavily at the thought of spending week upon week of boredom in a place where there was nothing to do. It was all the more frustrating when he thought about the ginormous task he and Mesmo were facing. And now he wasn't going to be able to do anything about it for a whole month.

Sure, it would be another two hundred years before the Toreq returned to Earth to judge whether the human race was worthy of survival, but there was so much to do!

In that time, humans would have to learn to live alongside animals, clean up their mess, stop sending more pollution into the air and the sea, drastically change their way of living and show more respect for their natural environment.

Just to name a few...

In the last couple of months, Ben had tried to offer himself as a bridge between humans and the rest of the animal kingdom. But that idea had failed.

He hadn't been able to communicate meaningfully with any animals at all. Either they had fled, or they were sick, or they avoided him at all costs. They didn't trust him. And with good reason.

Ben had seen firsthand the destruction left behind by greedy human hands. Why would animals ever want to trust one of his kind?

If the Toreq returned today, things would not go well.

This worrisome idea followed him as he exited the ferry and got on the packed bus.

He looked around, surprised anyone else would voluntarily travel to the end of the world. He checked for other teens who might be going to the same camp, but most were young adults, couples, or young families who seemed overly excited at being there.

Ben flopped onto an empty seat and stuck his face to the windowpane.

Crazy tourists.

He'd vaguely heard about Tofino being a tourist destination, but for the life of him, he couldn't remember why. It couldn't be because of the coastline, which was rocky, jagged, and extremely dangerous. It lay on the Pacific Rim, after all. The water there was cold, and currents could drag you under in the blink of an eye. Not exactly your typical beach vacation.

Maybe young adults went there to party away from their parent's eyes while couples spent entire evenings drooling over romantic sunsets.

Oh, yay. Just great.

Someone sat beside him. In no mood for a chat, Ben sank his head back in his chair and pretended to sleep.

He considered his grumpy mood and had to admit that Mesmo had been right. It wasn't that he had gotten up on the wrong side of the bed, or that he felt left out of the meeting Mesmo was going to have with the Wise Ones. Rather, it was his unsuccessful trips and lack of communication with the animal world that bothered him. He had imagined himself swooping in to save the day, convincing all that flew, crawled, and swam of his and Mesmo's great plan. He'd imagined enthusiastic, even welcoming reactions.

But none of this had happened, and with each failed attempt, he felt more and more drained, more and more useless. He'd thought he'd be the right one for the job. But what if he wasn't?

With this lingering thought in mind, Ben stepped off the bus onto the main street of Tofino three hours later. He checked his mom's instructions on a piece of paper. He was supposed to meet some guy named Wilson Maesschalck. The camp coordinator, he guessed.

M-a-e-s-s-c-h-a-l-c-k... How'm I even supposed to pronounce that?

The other travellers drifted off to their separate destinations. The bus took off with a roar of its engine.

Ben watched tourists line up for a late lunch at a popular-looking restaurant with a large terrace shaded by a tree that sprouted in the middle. Lively music played from loudspeakers. Five teenagers walked by, giggling and sipping on slurpees, wearing flip-flops and shorts. A couple of professional bikers slid down the street behind him. But there was no sign of an assembly of young campers. Nor a Wilson Maesschalck, for that matter.

Drat, now he'd have to call Mom.

And tell her about her brilliant camping plan...

"Ben!"

He glanced about, wondering who had called his name.

"Ben!" The voice came from much closer now.

He whirled, just in time to see a girl run up to him. She flung her arms around him so hard he almost lost his balance. Her long, black hair brushed against his face, smelling of pine needles and ocean air.

"I'm so glad you're here!" she squealed, squeezing him.

He took a step back, staring into the most wonderful pixie eyes. "Kimi?" he gasped in shock.

"Ta-da!" she cried, thrusting her arms apart as if she had just jumped out of a Christmas present, her flowery dress swirling. "Surprise!"

"Kimi?" he repeated, unable to believe that his best friend stood before him. "But... how... what..." he stammered. "What are you doing here?"

She laughed in reaction to his clueless face. "It's all part of a big *scheme*..." She gave him a mischievous look, and was about to say more, when someone shouted behind them, "Hey, Kimimela!"

Ben turned to find a strong-built young man with short, dark hair stride towards them.

"Did you find your boyfriend?"

Ben went crimson.

"He's *not* my boyfriend!" Kimi snapped.

The young man, who looked around twenty-five, crossed his tattooed arms over his chest. "Sure, he is." His eyes twinkled. "He's a *boy*, and he's your *friend. Boy-friend.* See?"

"Arrrgh!" Kimi roared, then said in a gruff voice, "This is Benjamin Archer, my *friend.*" She turned to Ben and, in a calmer tone, said, "Ben, this is my cousin Wilson..."

"...Messkalk..., Massk..." Ben blurted.

The young man's smile widened. "It's pronounced *Maasgalk*, with a soft 'g'. Finally, I get some long-deserved recognition around here. Nice to meet you, Ben-friend," he said, stretching out his hand and showing rows of white teeth. Ben couldn't help staring at the four-masted ship tattooed on the man's bicep.

Ben grinned as they shook hands, Wilson's grasp feeling firm and authentic. Sensing he could take part in the good-natured conversation, Ben asked with fake anger, "So, is somebody going to tell me what's going on around here?"

Kimi giggled. "It's our moms. They called each other to organize something for the summer. That's when my mom came up with this idea to send us both *camping.*" She drew invisible quotation marks in the air with her fingers. "Your mom didn't think it would work out, at first, but last week she changed her mind and said you could come. She said to keep it a surprise."

Ben's eyes widened. "So, there's no camping group?"

"Nope. You and I are staying with my mom's cousin, Auntie Jen and her husband Pieter, by the beach."

Wilson cleared his throat. "Hum-hum, and yours truly."

Kimi rolled her eyes. "Yes, and cousin Wil, here. He's visiting from the mainland. He's starting a Ph.D. in Oceanography at UBC[1] next fall."

"Cool!" Ben said, impressed.

"Yeah, yeah, enough flattery already." Wilson waved a dismissive hand at him. "Listen, kids, I gotta run some errand for Pa. I'll meet you back here in an hour, ok?"

Kimi nodded, then shouted to the receding cousin, "We'll be at the ice cream parlour!"

Wilson clicked his tongue and gave them the thumbs up.

"Come on," Kimi said, linking her arm with his and leading him across the street. "We can catch up over ice cream. Unless you'd rather get a

---

[1] UBC = University of British Columbia

sandwich?"

"Oh, no, no," Ben said hurriedly. "Ice cream will do." He felt all fuzzy inside and couldn't stop grinning. This could turn into an amazing summer after all, if he let it.

* * *

"You have no idea," Kimi said, pointing a long ice cream spoon at him. "What a lasting impression you left at the school. I mean, kids have this theory that a flock of crows entered the classroom and carried you away. You've become a legend."

Ben snorted as he stuffed his mouth with bubble gum flavour. "What about Wes and Tyler?" he asked. He still hadn't gotten used to seeing Kimi in a dress. He had only known her with black trousers, black shirts and black army boots. Now, she looked light and carefree.

Kimi nodded as if he had just asked a major question. "Ah, I meant to tell you. They have this impressive YouTube channel. I'll show you their videos later. They're quite good, actually."

Ben grinned. "And what about your mom? And Thomas?"

Kimi's face radiated. "She's doing great.

They're both doing great. Thomas moved in with us, did you know? Mom's so happy..." she trailed off, lost in thought.

Ben stared at her, imagining Kimi's pretty mother with her long, black hair and high cheekbones. "I'm really glad," he said earnestly, remembering the family's struggles.

"It was really hard for a while, you know?" Kimi said. "But Mom's healing every day. I'm so proud of her."

Ben smiled, realizing he'd been longing for some good news.

But Kimi's face faltered. "I'm sorry about Tike, Ben," she said. "Mom said you lost him. We were so worried about you. We had no idea if you'd made it across the mountain. But then your mom called and said you were ok."

Ben forgot about his ice cream. The sun warmed his cheeks, the town atmosphere lulled him, and he was still basking in the news of spending the summer with his best friend. He was not ready to think about Tike, lying in an icy coffin under heaps of snow.

"I'm sorry," Kimi said quickly as if willing her words away. "I shouldn't have said anything. We don't have to talk about it."

Ben opened his mouth, struggling to come

up with something to say.

"Hey, guys, where's mine?" a voice complained. Wilson slid into a chair at their table, staring at his nonexistent dessert.

"You said you'd be an hour!" Kimi burst. "I'm not leaving ice cream in the sun for an hour. Get one yourself!"

Wilson turned to look inside the ice cream parlour, then coughed and rubbed his hands on his pants' legs, as if he suddenly didn't need ice cream anymore.

Ben figured he didn't want to line up but found only a couple of customers waiting for their order.

"...or are you afraid of *Anna*?" Kimi teased.

"Who?" Wilson said innocently, turning to check the store counter again.

Kimi rolled her eyes at Ben.

Squinting inside the parlour, Ben noticed a pretty girl with blond, shoulder-length hair who looked to be about Wilson's age or a bit younger. She was wearing the parlour t-shirt and cap. Ben glanced at Kimi, who gave him a sideways smile.

She spoke to Wilson. "Anna. You know? From your high school?" Kimi stressed the words with exaggeration. "She's going to UBC in September, did you know that? You should talk to her, tell her what it's like."

Wilson stumbled over his words. "Ugh, I don't have time for that. We still have half an hour's drive to Craggy Bay. Pa's waiting for his lumber. And Ma is impatient to meet Ben-friend, here. We'd best be off if you're done with that." He pointed at Kimi's empty ice cream cup and stood without waiting for an answer.

Kimi pressed her lips together, then got up, hurrying after Wilson with Ben in tow. "Wait a minute, aren't you going to ask her to Friday's Summer Dance?"

Wilson humphed. "Me? At a dance? Don't be stupid." He walked away with large strides, forcing Ben and Kimi to trot behind him until they reached a pickup truck with a stack of lumber leaning on the side. Wilson unlocked the tailgate and said, "Here, Ben-friend, help me load. Let's build some muscles on those flimsy arms of yours."

Ben picked up a couple of lumber pieces and passed them on to Wil, then felt a tap on the shoulder.

"I'll be right back," Kimi whispered. She winked and sprinted off.

They were done loading five minutes later. Ben tossed his backpack beside the lumber and joined Wilson in the front. He was putting on his seatbelt when Kimi climbed into the pickup beside him, an ice cream cone in her hand.

"Here you go," she said cheerfully.

"For me?" Wilson said, accepting the dessert. "Hey, thanks, cousin!" He took a big bite and started the motor with his other hand.

"...and she said yes," Kimi shouted over the rumble.

Wilson almost choked. "She... *what?*"

Kimi stretched over and clapped a Post-it on Wilson's lap. "Anna said yes," Kimi repeated. "She wants to go to the Summer Dance with you. This is her address and phone number. You're picking her up at six."

Ben expected Wilson's hand to crush the ice-cream cone at any moment.

"I'm doing *what?*" the young man turned towards Kimi, eyes bulging.

Ben stiffened between them, looking straight ahead and willing himself to disappear into the car seat.

"Bye, Anna," Kimi shouted, ignoring Wilson and leaning out her window. "Wave," she growled over her shoulder at the boys.

Ben and Wilson saw the blond-haired girl wave at them from afar. "Bye, Wil!" they heard her shout.

Wilson waved mechanically, then sank back in his chair, arms outstretched over the steering wheel, ice cream dripping down his hand. He gobbled up the cone with two huge bites, then pressed the gas pedal, making the truck lurch forward. "You creep, you... How dare you...," he grumbled all the way out of town.

Kimi hummed while staring out the open window.

That's when Ben noticed Wilson furtively sneaking the Post-it into his shirt pocket.

* * *

"Benjamin, dear. Welcome," the petite woman said, hugging Ben as if she'd known him all his life. She wore a white, short-sleeved buttoned shirt, khaki trousers and sandals. She had simple pearl earrings and just a touch of makeup. Her dark hair was pulled up in a ponytail, giving her a youthful look, even though she must have been over fifty years old.

"Everybody calls him Ben, Auntie," Kimi said, hugging the woman. She turned to Ben. "This is my mother's distant cousin, Aunt Jeniece—or Auntie Jen. She moved to Craggy Bay long before I was born."

Auntie Jen smiled. "That's what happens when you find love," she said.

"What would I have done if you had said no?" a man said, appearing from behind the door and placing a hand on her shoulder. "Right, *schatje*[2]?"

Auntie Jen patted his hand. "This is Pieter Maesschalck," she said to Ben. "You can call him Uncle Pete if you like."

Uncle Pete's green eyes twinkled as he clasped Ben's hand. "Benjamin, *jongen*[3]! What took you so long? Was my son flirting with all the town girls again?"

Ben grinned sheepishly as he followed Kimi inside.

"Ha, ha, very funny, Pa," Wilson roared through the doorway behind them, though Ben found him smiling. Clearly, this was some kind of household joke, which he took lightly. Wilson dumped shopping bags on the kitchen counter and said, "Here's the groceries you asked for, Ma."

Auntie Jen kissed Wilson on the cheek.

---

[2] *Schatje* : Flemish for 'darling'. Literally: little treasure.

[3] *Jongen* : Flemish for 'boy' or 'son'.

"Things are so much easier when you're around," she said gratefully.

Wilson squeezed his mother's shoulders, then shouted across the room, "Make yourself useful, old man, and help me unload that lumber you ordered. The summer's not getting any longer, you know."

Uncle Pete laughed and clapped Ben on the back. "Welcome, Ben. Stay as long as you like."

Ben's heart bulged. He wasn't used to being received with such open-heartedness. "Thank you," he managed, choking a little.

Kimi must have noticed because she pulled him by the arm. "Come on, I'll show you your room. It fits two single beds. You'll have to share it with Wil, though. I hope you don't mind."

He didn't.

They passed through a comfortable living-room with antique-looking furniture, an open fireplace and bookshelves everywhere, stacked with leather-bound volumes. Ben had never seen so many books in a living-room before.

Small, oval paintings of what Ben took to be distant ancestors hung on the walls. Several miniature sailing ships adorned the sideboards, including a stunning replica of a four-masted ship that decked an upright piano. Ben recognized it. It was the same one as Wilson's tattoo.

"It's beautiful!" he said, admiring its details.

"You can say that again! Uncle Pete is one of the best miniature ship modelists in the world."

Ben stared wide-eyed at her as they headed up the stairs to the first floor.

"I've got my cousin Lori's old room," Kimi said, the steps creaking under her feet. "That's Auntie Jen's eldest daughter. She married last year and moved to Quebec."

"What did I tell you?" they heard Auntie Jen from the kitchen. "When you find love..."

Kimi shook her head apologetically. "Teasing is a way of life around here," she said. "You'll get used to it."

Ben grinned, knowing he would.

CHAPTER 7 *Broken Balance*

Jeremy Michaels pressed the phone to his ear.

A woman from the Canadian Security Intelligence Service—*CSIS* for short—spoke on the other end, "High Inspector Hao is unavailable at the moment. Would you like to leave a message?"

Jeremy seethed through his teeth. "I've left six messages already. My name is Jeremy Michaels—that's M-I-C-H-A-E-L-S. I'm a reporter with the Provincial Times. I'm writing an article about *The Cosmic Fall* and High Inspector James Hao's insights on the subject would be greatly appreciated."

The woman's tone remained neutral, making Jeremy feel like he was talking to an answering machine. "I have taken note. Thank you and have a good day." She hung up.

Jeremy stared at his smartphone, then thrust it on a pile of papers and photographs on his desk.

Drat!

He sighed, then threw his feet on the table next to his computer and bent his arms behind his neck to rest his head in his hands.

Actually, the more the National Aerial Division of the CSIS rejected him, the more intrigued he became.

Why were the secret services intent on burying the event that took place in Chilliwack? *The Cosmic Fall* was approaching its first anniversary—the perfect opportunity to release a full-fledged first-page recap—yet everybody seemed to have conveniently forgotten that it had ever occurred.

Only the Parks and Recreation Association had anything to say about the area where the meteors had crashed. They had politely mentioned a vague project to create an educational centre on the premisses. But even they had referred Jeremy back to the CSIS.

And then there were the mysterious disappearances of the neighbourhood's inhabitants. Well, not exactly 'disappearances', more like 'unavailability'. Of the four houses neighbouring the field where *The Cosmic Fall* had occurred, one inhabitant had landed himself in jail and wouldn't take his calls, one man was deceased, and two others had vanished off the face of the Earth.

Coincidence?

Maybe. Maybe not.

In fact, he had only been able to talk to two people so far: that woman and that kid.

Jeremy picked up a blurry photograph. It was the last picture he had taken before landing on his backside after the bee attack. He squinted at a cluster of shrubs and trees, an eerie glow (sunlight reflecting on something?), the swarm of bees, and there, in the shadows... Was that the boy's face?

"Hey, rookie, are you done yet?"

The voice pulled Jeremy from his thoughts. He slid his feet off the desk and straightened in his chair just before a colleague popped his head over the office space panel.

"The boss is waiting for your article, man. Are you almost done?"

Jeremy poured over his keyboard, looking busy. "Yup, yup, tell him five minutes."

The colleague pushed his reading glasses further up his nose and disappeared.

Jeremy stared at the title on his screen: CHILLIWACK'S ORGANIC BONANZA. The rest of the page was blank.

* * *

Ben and Kimi stepped out of the house the next day to find a foggy morning.

Auntie Jen and Uncle Pete's spacious home lay nestled among the well-adapted environment of the rugged Pacific Coast. Craggy Bay's single road led to a dead end on one side, while the other side reached Tofino.

Kimi had given Ben one of Wilson's old wetsuits, while she wore one that Lori had left behind. She led Ben into a workshop at the back of the weatherbeaten house and uncovered a couple of old surfboards, which had clearly been used often, judging from their faded colour. They dusted off the cobwebs, then headed down a narrow path to Craggy Bay Beach—one of the few sandy beaches along the coast. It was bordered by thick shrubbery and spindly trees, twisted from years of ocean winds.

When they reached the end of the path and Ben stepped on the freezing grey sand, he looked up and gasped. The rising sun bathed the mist that clung to the beach in a ghostly yellow light, and as they walked further, the mist closed in on them, so only sand and waves were visible.

Then, black dots began to appear on the waves. Ben squinted, realizing he was looking at other surfers, and it dawned on him why this tiny place at the edge of the ocean was such a coveted tourist destination.

Surfing!

Ben's heart soared.

It wasn't just Kimi and him who were heading into the ice-cold water. The beaches around Tofino were known for their surfing, and on a worldwide level at that! The rugged coast and head-on Pacific weather meant huge waves hit the beaches. And this was not some small pastime for locals, far from it. Ben was looking at full-fledged, international-level surfing crowds.

Fortunately, Craggy Bay had one of the calmer beaches. It lay nestled in a half-circle that protected the beach from the biggest waves and allowed beginners to give the sport a try.

Kimi turned to look at him, and the same excitement reflected in her eyes. "Race you!" she shouted, sprinting away, the surf-board clinging under her arm.

"Hey!" Ben objected, bolting after her.

They reached the group of surfers, some of whom had been there since dawn, and squealed as their feet splashed into the freezing waters of the north. It wasn't long, though, before their wetsuits came into action, protecting them with a layer of water that warmed up in contact with their skin.

For a moment, Ben allowed himself not to think about his troubles, to ignore the skill, and spend hour upon hour of fun trying to surfboard on his stomach close to shore.

The mist cleared, and the sun soared high until the two friends trudged out of the water and sprawled on the hot sand, gasping for breath.

They giggled with exhaustion, their surfboards thrust aside, their arms and legs outstretched on the sand. Several minutes passed, where Ben stared at seagulls and felt the sand warm his back. And before he could help himself, he said, "Thanks, Kimi."

She kept her eyes closed as she soaked up the sun. "For what?"

He paused for a moment, then said, "For not asking any questions."

She opened her eyes, then rolled on her side to face him. "It's your mom. She said you'd been through a rough time and that it would really help if you could forget about everything for a while."

Ben squinted at the sunlight, listening to her words.

"Is it working?" she asked.

Ben bit his bottom lip, thinking about his outburst back home, then nodded.

She considered him for a while, then sank on to her back again. "Good."

They stared at the blue sky for a while, then Kimi ventured, "I'd still like to know about that crow invasion. And about Mesmo. And about those men who were after you. And about what happened to Tike..." Her hand brushed his shoulder. "But only when you're ready."

Ben couldn't trust himself to talk, so he nodded without taking his eyes off a cloud.

Kimi dropped her hand back in the sand. "And there's something else I'd like to know," she added.

Ben frowned. "What's that?"

She rolled onto her side, her sand-filled braid plastered against her wet suit. "Are you sure you've never surfed before?"

Ben grinned and shook his head. "No, never."

Kimi nodded in approval. "Well, I'd never have guessed. You were pretty good out there for a first-timer."

Ben felt a sneaky smile creep up the corner of his mouth. "Thanks," he said. "You weren't too bad yourself. Except when you fell headfirst in the water the first couple of times."

"Hey! You fell, too!" she objected, throwing a handful of sand at him.

That set them off, running and dodging each other's sand bullets with the surfboards under their arms until their growling stomachs forced them home. By the time they reached the path that led to the house, Ben felt like he was facing Mount Everest. He groaned with each footstep and slapped at mosquitoes on his neck. The wetsuit had suddenly become unbearable in the midday heat.

The house looked like a haven of freshness, and delicious smells came from the open kitchen window.

Wilson and Uncle Pete were hammering away next to the workshop, building something.

Uncle Pete took some nails out of his mouth. "Hey, there, son, when you're done with lunch, we could do with an extra pair of hands."

Ben stopped and swayed a little. "Er... sure, Uncle Pete."

Wilson sent him a wink, while Kimi chortled into her hand.

Ben curled his nose at her.

"What?" she said. "Did you think you were on vacation or something?"

* * *

Ben worked all afternoon beside Wilson and Uncle Pete, who wanted to build a new workshop for his miniature boats because the old one had become too unstable.

While they worked, Uncle Pete explained how he came from a long line of Flemish sailors who originated from Bruges, located in the European country of Belgium. That was where his Flemish name *Maesschalck* came from.

"Eight centuries ago, Bruges was a bustling harbour. Its glory lasted for five hundred years, but when sand filled the mouth of the river, the town became inaccessible, and it fell into oblivion. Today, its untouched medieval streets and canals have turned it into a major European tourist destination," Uncle Pete said, wiping his sweating forehead.

"During the Second World War, Bruges was occupied by German soldiers. My father was a Flemish shipbuilder who fought with the resistance. But when Canadian soldiers set the city free, my father was badly hurt in the cross-fire. A Canadian nurse took care of him. You can guess what happened next. They fell in love and fled war-torn Europe, pledging to live a quiet life back in Canada. That's how they eventually ended up in Tofino, where I was born." He stepped back to make sure he had placed his piece of lumber straight, then bent to pick up another one.

"Jen and I have often travelled to Bruges. She even learned Flemish with me! Its history fascinates us, with its old belfry, cobbled streets, lace weavers and antique bookstores. Did you know that the very first book in the English language was published there six hundred years ago?"

Wilson whispered behind his hand at Ben, "Hence the book-hoarding."

Ben grinned, thinking of the book-laden shelves inside the house.

Uncle Pete pointed a finger at Ben. "So, you see? From a tiny place along the Northern Sea to a tiny place on the Pacific Coast... You never know what life will throw at you, Ben. You'll understand what I mean when you're older."

Ben stopped hammering and stared at Uncle Pete.

They spent the evening chatting over a

hearty dinner of *chicon au gratin* and fries. At first, Ben tried to figure out this traditional Belgian dish made from a weird-looking vegetable covered in a delicious cheesy sauce, but the truth was he could barely keep his eyes open.

Auntie Jen noticed and released him to bed.

He accepted gladly and crashed into bed on his stomach, the softness of the bedsheets feeling heavenly under his cheek.

His muscles hurt, his face was sunburnt, and he had hit a finger with a hammer. But he was happier than he had been in a long while.

And now he understood what his mother had meant when she had said he needed to take a break, have fun, and forget about the skill for a while.

"She was right," he breathed into the pillow.

"What's that?"

Ben opened an eye to find Wilson putting on his nightshirt.

"Oh, nothing," Ben said with an effort. He was already drifting away.

Wilson sat on the edge of his bed and stared at Ben. "You did a good job today, helping my Pa out like that. You're a good kid, you know."

Ben opened an eye again, caught off guard by the compliment. "It's nothing, really," he mumbled, his words muffled by the cushion.

Wilson switched off the light, and glorious darkness filled the room.

"'Night, Ben-friend," Wilson said through a yawn.

"'Night, Wil."

* * *

The weeks passed in a similar fashion: surfing, putting together the workshop, strolling around Tofino with an ice cream cone in hand, hiking the rugged trails and going to the movies to watch *Galaxy Hero*.

Auntie Jen and Kimi practically pushed Wilson out of the house when the night of the Summer Dance came. They would not hear of him cancelling his date with the ice cream parlour girl. Ben watched as they fussed over him. He couldn't understand why Kimi and her aunt spent a whole hour trying to figure out which trousers and shirt he should wear, making him change three times.

"You're so weird," Ben mouthed at Kimi.

She rolled her eyes at him, then thrust another shirt in Wilson's hands.

Uncle Pete had washed the pickup truck

inside and out, so it looked almost brand new. Wilson had no choice; he trudged heavily to the truck and roared away without uttering a single word.

No sooner had the truck disappeared behind the bend, when Uncle Pete barked, "Well, what are you waiting for? Everybody in the car, we've got a Summer Dance to attend."

They packed into the four-seater and headed into town, where they spent a festive evening strolling around animated streets, watching fireworks, and even making silly attempts at swinging to the music.

Ben was fast asleep by the time Wilson returned. He woke long enough to mumble, "How'd it go?"

"None of your business, nosy-head," Wilson growled in a low voice, but he turned to Ben with a curious smile on his face and Ben thought he winked.

The next afternoon, Wilson invited them to go fishing. When Kimi and Ben arrived at the small pier, they found not only Wilson but Anna as well, waiting for them.

This last activity was less to Ben's liking until he discovered that Kimi's cousin was a fountain of information on local wildlife. Being a marine biologist and oceanographer, he knew everything there was to know about local fish and wildlife, and Ben soaked up every ounce of information like a sponge.

As the four of them sped off in the small motorboat, crisscrossing through a string of jutting islands, Ben eyed Kimi suspiciously.

How did she know?

As if he had spoken aloud, she looked at him, her long fringe slapping the side of her face, her black hair dancing in the wind at her back, and gave him a knowing smile.

There wasn't much time to mull about it further, because Wilson pointed out a black bear with its two cubs strolling along a rocky beach, then a lonely wolf, some seals, and several kinds of seabirds. The animals did not try to communicate with Ben, nor he with them. All went about their life in this abundant place. Ben was relieved that such a pristine area still existed in the world. He promised himself, however, that he would attempt to communicate with the creatures before his vacation was over.

But not now. Not just yet.

Now, he was just a normal boy, enjoying a normal vacation surrounded by friends.

His thoughts popped like a bubble when

Wilson hauled in a massive salmon. It flopped around the boat, its gills protruding. Wilson ended its pain, then knelt beside the fish for an unusual amount of time.

Ben frowned at Kimi.

Wilson turned to them, his face grim. "There once was a balance between the hunter and the hunted. But modern man has broken that balance. We have become so far removed from the natural life-cycle, that we have forgotten where our food comes from.

He stared at the salmon. "We have cut ourselves from the food chain, which holds everything in place, and now that balance is lost."

Ben stared at Kimi's cousin. Unbeknown to him, Wilson couldn't have laid out Ben's mission more clearly: he had to mend life's broken balance.

It started to drizzle, so they headed back to shore, lost in thought.

That night, under drumming rain, Ben ate the best fish in his life. He realized that it wasn't that humans should stop eating animals because all creatures on Earth ate other creatures or were eaten themselves. The problem was that humans had disrupted the food chain, becoming its sole master. No one wanted to think about the fact that pesticides killed hundreds of insects, that cutting forests for industrial-sized crops eliminated biodiversity that had taken millions of years to thrive, that cooping fifty hens in one cage to save space was an inhuman practice...

If he could get animals to talk to him and he could transmit their grievances to the human world, then the healing could begin, and together, they could find a way to restore that balance.

"Earth to Ben, Earth to Ben," Kimi said beside him at the dinner table.

"Huh? Oh, sorry. I was thinking about what Wil said earlier on the boat."

She nodded. "I know. Wil has this ability to make people wonder about things. I think it's because of his ancestors, you see. I mean, Uncle Pete's family has always lived on the coast and sailed the oceans. He and Wil understand the bond between the land and the sea like no one else. It's in their blood."

A window crashed open in the kitchen, blowing wind and rain inside and making Auntie Jen yelp in surprise.

Uncle Pete rushed to close it. "Whew! We've got quite the storm brewing. We might as well get comfortable by the fire. Who wants Belgian chocolate?"

"Me!" everyone shouted in chorus.

The five of them settled in the living room with steaming cups topped with melting marshmallows. Ben hadn't even had time to notice that the Maesschalck had no television. Come to think of it, they didn't even have smartphones—except for the one Wilson had tossed on his bedroom dresser, and which hadn't moved since Ben had arrived. When Ben had pointed out that the battery was dead, Wilson had shrugged, pointed to his family and said, "I have all the social media I need right here." If they needed anything, they could just walk to one of the neighbours and ask for a helping hand.

"Ma," Wilson said. "Tell us a story. I miss your stories when I'm on campus."

Ben stared at him, surprised that the tough man would ask his mother for a story.

But Kimi jumped in, "Yes, please, Auntie Jen. Pick a story for us."

Ben watched Auntie Jen sip on her cup of steaming chocolate, while Wilson added some logs to the fire. She smiled peacefully as if she had done this a thousand times.

"*Schatje*, will you get me the Fables, please?" she asked Uncle Pete, who smiled and nodded.

He unlocked the glass-paned door of an oak

book-case, where only a handful of books were put on special display. When he carefully removed a gilt-edged tome with a thick leather cover, Ben knew he was being treated to something special.

Uncle Pete handed the heavy book to Auntie Jen, who rested it on her knees and turned its pages as if they were made of breakable glass.

"Jen is an expert in antique books, Ben. She has travelled far and wide buying and selling them." Uncle Pete said. "This one, in particular, is a compilation of the Fables of La Fontaine, a French author from the seventeenth century. He wrote short stories about animals that teach a moral."

"Ma, treat Ben to one that he won't find in the bookstores," Wilson said.

Auntie Jen nodded. "That's what I was thinking, too." She turned to Ben. "These Fables are studied in schools all over the world, Ben. But some stories in this old English translation... Well, you won't find them printed anywhere else. Only a handful of people in the world know about them, which makes them so unique."

Eyes widening, Ben settled on his stomach on the carpet beside Kimi, sipped on his hot chocolate, and listened.

CHAPTER 8 *The Orca and the Moon*

"A long time ago, before humans roamed the land, many orcas lived in the sea. They were pure-black in colour and loved to play and bask in the sunlight," Auntie Jen read. "A young orca named Humblefin was very curious. He asked questions about everything and wanted to know why there was a white ball in the night sky. He wanted to play with it.

"The black orca family became obsessed with the white ball, and all wished to play with it. They learned to leap out of the water, higher and higher. Tournaments were held, and strong, young orca-men competed to leap and swing with their tails in the hopes of kicking the white ball out of the sky.

"Humblefin's brother, Proudfin, dreamt of being the winner of the tournament. But he was too heavy and too lazy to leap out of the water. So, he decided to cheat. He had seen land with a mountain that reached for the clouds. He thought, "If I can reach the top of that mountain, I can kick the white ball out of the sky.

"Humblefin told him, "Don't do it, brother. It is not in our nature to go on the land." But Proudfin was secretly jealous of Humblefin, who was the best leaper among the black orca, and did not listen.

"So Proudfin went to the land and began to crawl forward. But he was too heavy, and he was not made for the land, and so he died. His spirit separated from his body, unable to move on to the Land of the Dead. "This is all my brother's fault," his spirit thought. "If my brother had not been such a good leaper, I would have won the tournament, and I would not have had to come on the land." His evil spirit turned into a black owl that watched the sea with envy.

"In the meantime, something miraculous happened. Humblefin, who was taking part in the tournament, and who had practiced his leap for months on end, knew with certainty that the white ball would be his. He swam with his strong tail up through the ocean, then leapt out of the water. Some said he looked so graceful they thought he could fly. He swirled in the air and kicked the white ball out of the sky.

"All looked on in wonder and waited for Humblefin to recover his prize. Humblefin swam to The Edge of the Ocean, where the white ball had fallen, and discovered something very strange. The ball unfurled and turned into a beautiful, white orca-woman. They fell in love instantly.

"Proudfin, whose spirit now inhabited the owl, felt rage at his brother's success. "The white orca-woman will be mine," Owl thought as he swooped down from the sky. He swept the white orca-woman and the black orca-man under his wings. But they were too heavy, and Humblefin fought back.

"If the orca-woman cannot be mine, then she will not be yours, either," Owl told Humblefin, and in a last effort, hurled orca-woman back into the sky, while he and his brother fell into the sea, where Owl drowned.

"Humblefin was inconsolable. He swam in circles in the sea, while orca-woman watched in sadness from above. Yet, white orca-woman had left something with Humblefin. He was no longer pure-black. He became a beautiful combination of black and white. And Humblefin had left something with her. She was no longer a white ball in the sky, but a beautiful combination of light and dark. The other orca looked on at her in wonder and called her Lady Moon.

"Many times, Humblefin tried to kick Lady Moon out of the sky, so they could be together again. But he had become old and did not have his former strength.

"Today, still, the orcas leap out of the water in honour of Lady Moon. They say that, sometimes, when the half-moon touches The Edge of the Ocean, Humblefin and Lady Moon can finally be together again for a brief time. And that," Auntie Jen finished, "is how the orca and the moon got their colour."

* * *

Rain thundered on the roof. Kimi, Wilson and Uncle Pete remained quiet, watching the flames in the fireplace. Ben stared at Auntie Jen. Her eyes were set in the distance as if she could personally remember the time when the story had occurred.

Ben sipped on his cup, only to find he had already emptied it. His mind flipped as he tried to make sense of the tale. "So, how..." he began, wondering what he wanted to say. His mind burst with questions.

Auntie Jen smiled at him encouragingly.

"So..." Ben tried again. "I don't get it. How can the moon turn into an orca-woman or a spirit into an owl?"

"You are looking at facts, Ben," Auntie Jen said. "But that is not what this story is about. You should search for meaning instead."

Ben frowned and looked at Kimi.

"What you want to know is: what do the orca represent, and what is the meaning of the owl?" Kimi said. She got off her stomach and sat cross-legged with her back straight. "Lady Moon is imagination, Humblefin is determination. When they work together, wonderful new things are created.

"Proudfin is laziness. Owl is envy and greed. These are emotions that destroy creativity, and we should be wary of them."

Ben stared at her with his mouth open. "And you know this... how?"

Wilson laughed and said, "You need to come out here more often, Ben-friend."

* * *

The wind tore at his body, pelting him with thick raindrops. Night enveloped him. How was it that he now stood with his feet in freezing water?

What am I doing out on the beach in the middle of the storm?

Ben searched the darkness, panic gripping him. Had he not been talking about Auntie Jen's story, just moments ago? He spotted a light from one of the windows of Uncle Pete's house. Twisted branches lashed at it like giant claws, hiding it from view.

Ben made to run, eager to return to safety, but found his feet stuck in the soggy sand. And his body felt heavy, so heavy. No matter how hard he fought to run towards the house, the wind and rain kept pinning him down. Cold sand grasped at his body like sticky fingers. Thick, black clouds swirled above. Waves crashed on the shore. Branches creaked.

But above all that racket, another sound emerged: it was a grinding noise, like scratching metal. It came from somewhere in the darkness, from the sea. It came from something massive, something *alive*. It breathed, in and out, in time with the waves. And it approached.

"Uncle Pete!" Ben cried, searching frantically for help. "Kimi!"

What madness had sent him outside on his own?

The beast ground its chains and snorted with hideous anger. Ben watched helplessly as the dark mass advanced towards him. Rain battered his face, drenching him.

Lighting crackled through the sky, illuminating the terrifying beast: twisted black feathers and gleaming yellow eyes.

The owl!

"The owl! The owl!" he shouted in terror, willing his voice to carry to the coasts' inhabitants, so they could flee.

The owl rose from the waves and bore down on him, dagger-like claws grabbing his shoulders.

"The owl! The..."

Ben gasped and sat straight up. Wilson's room. Uncle Pete's house. Fresh, ocean air seeping through the half-open window. A beam of warm, morning sunlight illuminating the back wall.

"Ben, are you ok?" Wilson's voice came through to him. He let go of the boy's shoulders.

Ben blinked several times, trying to shake off the fear that clung to his brain. His ears rang as though he'd been standing next to loudspeakers in a deafening concert.

I'm safe.

It had only been a dream.

"You had a nightmare," Wilson confirmed. "And it sounded like a bad one, too." He got off Ben's bed and began putting on his t-shirt. "Must've been the storm. It sure shook the house a good deal. I'm on my way out with Pa to check if there's any damage." He put an arm through the strap of his suspenders, then froze in mid-action. His eyes filled with an incredulous stare.

Ben lifted his hands to his hair to massage his throbbing head but stopped when he caught Wilson's baffled look.

What's up with him?

And then it hit him. Ben recognized the rushing sound in his ears, the silent whispers in his brain... Stomach roiling, he lowered his hands and saw the blue glow that hovered around his fingers.

The skill!

He clasped his hands together and shoved them into his lap in a clumsy attempt to hide them.

But it was too late. Wilson had seen the anomaly. He stared at Ben, eyebrows squished together, then mechanically proceeded to adjust his suspenders again. "Auntie Maggie," he said, deep in thought. "–Kimi's mother—she warned my Ma and Pa about you. She said you were… special. Pa says you're a *Dierenfluisteraar.*" He nodded to himself as if that sounded about right. "Yeah," he muttered. "You must be a *Dierenfluisteraar.*" He picked up the car keys and shoved them in his pocket, then lifted his eyes to meet Ben's and said, "It's ok, Ben-friend. Your secret is safe with me."

They stared at each other. Then Wilson whirled and disappeared through the door.

CHAPTER 9 *Beaching*

Ben dressed in a hurry, mind whirling.

What am I going to do about Wil?

He wanted to run after Wilson, come up with some lame excuse to make sure the man wasn't going to mention anything to anyone about what he had seen. But he had to wait several minutes because the skill played tricks on him. His hands glowed, yet he could not figure out which creature was trying to communicate with him. His mind filled with a confusing murmur, like static from a radio that struggled to connect to a radio station.

Once he'd managed to absorb the skill somewhat, he put on his hoodie, stuffed his hands in its front pockets, and headed downstairs, trying to ignore the cold sweat on his forehead.

He found Kimi at the breakfast table, Auntie Maggie bustling in the kitchen and Uncle Pete with a coffee jug in his hand. "There's no coffee!" he complained, lifting the lid and peeking inside.

There was no sign of Wilson.

"Morning, sleepyhead," Kimi said as Ben slipped into the chair next to her. She gestured with her head towards her uncle. "The storm knocked out the electricity: no coffee, no waffles, no lights."

"Poor dears," Auntie Jen said, ignoring her husband and serving Ben a bowl of cereal. "Did that storm keep you awake last night?"

"I slept fine, Auntie Jen," Kimi said, then glanced Ben's way. "Not sure about Ben, though. I bet he still can't make head or tail out of the Moon and Orca story."

Auntie Jen chuckled.

Ben blinked at his bowl.

"Aren't you going to eat that?" Kimi asked, watching him curiously.

Ben's stomach flipped.

"Pa!" Wilson's warning voice carried from outside.

The four of them turned toward the front door, which swung open.

"Pa!" Wilson shouted again, rushing inside. "The workshed's down!"

"What?" Ben gasped, jumping out of his seat. He and Uncle Pete exchanged a glance, then hurried outside.

And there it was, their beautiful new workshed: its walls and roof lying shattered on the ground under a fallen tree.

"Oh, no!" Ben exclaimed, heart sinking. For a minute, he forgot about the rushing sound in his ears.

We worked so hard!

Uncle Pete and Wilson inspected the damage. Auntie Jen and Kimi commented on the broken branches and leaves strewn around the house.

"Do you hear that?" Kimi frowned.

Throngs of shouting voices rose from the beach.

"I wonder what's going on?" Auntie Jen said.

A handful of people appeared next to the house, ushering each other down the path. "Hurry, hurry!" they shouted.

"Pieter!" the last one yelled as he ran past. "We need your help. Come quickly!" The urgency in the neighbour's voice made Ben's stomach lurch.

Uncle Pete sprang into action. "Something happened on the beach! Let's go! Quick!"

A wave of crippling fear gripped Ben's mind as if he were thrust back into his nightmare in broad daylight. He scrambled after the man with an overwhelming sense of foreboding.

The coastline was shrouded in a humid mist. The ground was littered with branches and garbage, like fishing nets and corroded metal plates from boats—things the ocean had tossed to shore.

But the ocean had vomited more than garbage onto the beach.

Ben watched in a daze as neighbours flocked to the shore. They ran past him, shouting and yelling. But Ben did not hear them. He heard something else, something that came from his mind, something captured by his senses like a well-positioned satellite dish.

Kimi shouted his name from somewhere far away. He saw concern on her face as her eyes went from his glowing hands to the massive dark boulders strewn on the beach.

Only, they weren't boulders. They were alive, and they spewed air through their blowholes.

Ben fell to his knees in the cold sand, his

body suddenly weighing a thousand tons.

"Ben!" Kimi yelled through the despair that assailed his mind. "What's wrong? Ben!"

He barely noticed as she tried to help him up. He managed to half-crawl, half-run to the first orca that had been thrust onto the beach. He placed his hands on the thick skin of the black-and-white killer whale, absorbing its heart-shattering scream with his whole being. The force thrust him back into the sand in shock.

Kimi tugged him by the arm.

He struggled to his feet again and approached the next orca, and then the next, and the next.

The sun rose, lifting the mist, revealing the extent of the catastrophe: not three, not ten, but *fifteen* killer whales, stuck in the sand.

Ben grabbed Kimi's arm and gazed at her with the eyes of a madman. "Pain!" he gasped. "So much pain!"

The whale's anguished cries crippled Ben. The human in him understood the urgency of the situation: immediate action was required. But his alien side had lost control of the skill. The door to his mind lay wide open, and the whales' despair became his as if he were the one lying at death's door.

Get a grip!

Mesmo had told him multiple times to watch out for this. He could lose himself to the skill, his mind and body becoming one with the animal, which could lead to a fatal end.

He closed his eyes and focused on untangling his thoughts from those of the orca.

I am Ben.

He scanned his human body, feeling lighter by the second.

"Ben?" Kimi said close to him.

He opened his eyes and found tears streaming down her face.

"We've got to get them back to the sea," he gasped.

"I know. But how?"

"Come," he said, taking her by the hand and running past a female orca. She must have been the biggest of them all because her tail stuck further into the water than the others.

He reached out and touched the side of the killer whale, feeling thick barnacles under his hand. The orca's black eye followed him.

My name is Benjamin Archer. What is yours?

I am Kana'kwa. Please, help! Help my pod!

The voice boomed in Ben's head, making

him step back as if he'd been thrust aside by a gust of wind. Undeterred, he returned by the killer whale's side.

I will get you and your family back into the water, I promise.

Hurry! We will not survive for long.

Ben stepped back again, this time because helplessness gripped him, but he did not want the orca to know. He clenched his fists. This was no time to show weakness.

Kana'kwa, tell me what to do.

CHAPTER 10 *Ticking Time*

"Get the strongest ropes and chains you can find. Bring your boats as close to shore as you can," Uncle Pete barked at a large group of neighbours who gathered around him. "We'll tie the ropes to their tails and try and drag them out."

One neighbour shook his head. "It's not going to work, Pieter. Have you seen the size of those things?"

"We have to try," Ben cried, breaking into the circle. "We can start with the youngest one. In the meantime, the others need water and shade. Bring towels, blankets, anything that absorbs water, and lay them on the orcas' backs. Get buckets and spray them with seawater!"

He turned to Uncle Pete, ignoring the

curious stares from the other adults. "We need to call in help from Tofino. Or better still, from the mainland. Maybe the navy can help. We need to get the orcas back in the water as soon as possible."

Uncle Pete reached for Ben's shoulders and led him aside. *"Jongen, jongen,"* he repeated in amazement. "You are incredibly resourceful, but the storm knocked out our communications. Our phones are dead, and the road to Tofino is cut off because of fallen trees."

Ben's eyes widened in alarm.

"It's ok," Uncle Pete added. "This happens all the time. The West Coast is known for its storms. It's a way of life here. We already have a team of people in place whose task it is to clear the road as soon as the weather allows it."

"Pieter, so what do we do?" a man spoke up, calling them back into the circle.

Uncle Pete straightened. "We do exactly as the boy says. Call all able-handed neighbours to the beach. Find your ropes and buckets and towels. Bring sunscreen, hats and water bottles for yourselves. This is going to be a long day. We can't afford to deal with dehydration and sunburns as well."

Everyone nodded and headed off in different directions.

Time wore on, and by late afternoon, with everyone's aid and assistance from three fishing boats, they managed to drag the youngest orca into deeper waters. Only, once there, it began to thrash frantically as it tried to swim back to its mother.

People risked getting seriously hurt by placing themselves between the young orca and the beach, but that only panicked it further.

Even Ben could not reason with it. Every time he made a cautious attempt at calling forth his skill, the whale's distress flooded his thoughts, rendering him useless.

Can't do it! I just can't...

"Enough!" Uncle Pete shouted. "It's no use, we're only making it weaker."

Everyone stepped back, t-shirts and shorts wet, faces haggard.

And that had only been the smallest and lightest orca...

Ben watched on, trying not to give in to panic.

Kimi locked hands with him and rested her forehead on his shoulder. Her hair smelled of sea salt.

"We need more people," Ben said. "We need trucks and stronger boats."

"But how?" she asked. "We don't have any of those."

Ben puffed his cheeks, then said, "Come on, I've got an idea."

They ran to Uncle Pete.

"There aren't enough of us. We need more people. We need the tourists!" Ben said.

Uncle Pete's eyes narrowed. "Hm, that's a smart idea. Only, the tourists are in Tofino, and we can't get there."

"Aren't the roads cleared yet?"

Uncle Pete shook his head and squeezed Ben's arm. "I'm sorry, *jongen*. We're going to have to call it a day. We did everything we could, but as you can see, we simply don't have the manpower to make a difference. We will try again tomorrow."

"No way! We have to keep trying. We can't afford to stop now. We can dig paths in the sand behind the orca, maybe they'll slide back. And we have to keep their skin wet..."

"Son," Uncle Pete said, taking him gently by the shoulders to stop his tirade. He waited until Ben was calm enough to look at him. "We did everything we could. But now we need to rest, so we can come back strengthened by sunrise tomorrow."

Ben's throat welled. The orcas' cries echoed painfully in his brain.

"I'm sorry, son," Uncle Pete said, his features downturned. "You worked hard. I'm proud of you. But it's time to go home."

Kimi glanced at Ben.

"No," he said, head stooped. "I'm staying. I'll stay here all night if I have to. I can't leave them."

"I'll stay with you," Kimi offered.

Ben sent her a grateful smile.

After managing to swallow some spaghetti, cooked over a portable propane burner, Ben and Kimi headed back to the beach with sleeping bags swung over their shoulders.

For about an hour after dark, they continued to hurl buckets of seawater at the orca, even if it barely covered a fraction of their gigantic bodies.

"Hey, guys," someone yelled from further up the beach. It was Wilson and Anna. They had placed their own sleeping bags next to Ben and Kimi's. "Come on," Wilson said, approaching them and reaching for their buckets. "Get some rest. We'll take over."

Ben almost cried with relief. "Thanks," he managed, too exhausted to say anything else.

"Ben-friend." Wilson stopped him. "You sleep now, ok? Word is spreading. More help will come. And I'll drive you into town myself tomorrow morning. We'll get ourselves some fresh tourists. How about that?"

Ben grinned and nodded, then dragged himself up the beach and crashed on to his sleeping bag without even closing the zipper.

* * *

He woke up early, his body sore from the tough labour of the previous day and the hard ground he had slept on. The others lay fast asleep beside him.

The sky glowed a marine blue, announcing the coming of sunrise and a beautiful day. But a beautiful day was not what they needed right now. Clear skies meant a scorching sun, a deadly element for the orca.

Ben trudged down to Kana'kwa, who lay suffering helplessly in the sand. Ben's eyes filled with tears. He couldn't help it. The transmitted pain felt too raw, even if he had managed to pull up protective barriers in his mind. He picked up the bucket, stepped into the freezing waves and filled it with water. He returned and gently bathed the whale's skin, knowing full well it was far from enough.

Thank you, Benjamin Archer.

The whale's voice had lost much of its strength.

Hang in there, Kana'kwa. Help is coming.

Kana'kwa answered with silence.

Ben continued to bathe the killer whale, taking note of every scar that ornamented her skin. And he discovered that each had a story: an encounter with a toothy sea creature, a collision with the propellers of a boat, a bump with a sharp rock while chasing for seals too close to shore... Kana'kwa had travelled more miles across the oceans than Ben could ever have imagined, from north to south and back again; and from the surface of the sea to the farthest depths of the ocean floor. Ben could only begin to guess the killer whale's great age, and he lamented this terrible ending.

Why? Why did you come to shore?

Kana'kwa's thoughts darkened in answer.

We were chasing salmon. But then the salmon disappeared as if a beast had gobbled them up in one bite. A beast greater than us.

In his mind, Ben heard the sound of grating claws and deep groans; a dark creature breathing in and out, in time with the waves. He shuddered in recognition.

Kana'kwa continued:

We became confused. We were afraid, and we fled, but the land caught us.

Ben thought about Kana'kwa's words. Something was out there, something massive and evil.

Other orca stirred in his mind, and the cries of pain began. Ben directed soothing thoughts at them as he noticed a pale moon dipping behind the fir trees behind him, leaving way for the sun.

Listen. I will tell you a story. It is the story of Humblefin and Lady Moon...

He wasn't sure how much of the story they would understand, but it felt like the right time to tell it, and all the while, he pondered on the fact that Auntie Jen had conveniently told this tale only two days ago. She couldn't have known that this was going to happen, could she?

By the time he was finished telling it, Ben found Kimi, Wilson, and Anna waiting for him by the sleeping bags. He didn't think about hiding his glowing hands this time, and they did not ask any questions.

"Let's go," Wilson said, leading them solemnly to the pickup truck.

CHAPTER 11 *Cornered*

"Where is Einar?" Mesmo asked impatiently. He put his hands on his hips and glanced across the cornfields to the house.

Amaru, who had been sitting peacefully on a log with his leather hands resting on his knees, said, "Einar arrived in Vancouver this morning. His plane from Oslo landed at dawn."

Mesmo shook his head, dissatisfied. "I don't understand. It's not in any Wise One's habit to arrive late. What's delaying him?"

The Bolivian native looked up at Mesmo. "Einar has not been *delayed*, Mesmo. No. Do not kid yourself. Einar is *stalling*."

Mesmo stared at Amaru, realizing the Wise One was right.

Amaru continued, "Do not expect anything from Einar, *amigo[4]*. He is not in favour of this irregular meeting you are holding. You may be able to sway us to your cause, but Einar is a whole other matter."

Mesmo turned and stared at the other five Wise Ones who had gathered in a circle under a giant maple tree. Crickets chirped in the summer heat, the cornfields basked in the sun, and insects buzzed in the haze. He sighed, "I cannot start the meeting without him. It is against the rules."

Amaru gazed at the rolling hills. "Yes. And Einar knows this all too well."

* * *

Ben, Kimi, Wilson and Anna squeezed into the front of the pickup truck and headed down the main road leading to Tofino. No one spoke. No one dared admit that the orca would probably never return to the sea. But they had to do whatever they could, right to the end.

Their progress was hampered by branches that littered the road, and one time they had to stop for ten minutes as a cleaning team removed a

[4] Amigo = Spanish word meaning 'friend'.

thick log that blocked the way. But they made it into town, eventually.

"Right," Wilson said as he parked the truck. "I'm going to find a couple of busses to transport people to the beach. Ben, do you think you could talk up the tourists to come and help? Check out the hotels, they must be having breakfast by now. Tell them to be at the main square by ten. Anna, Kimi: I need you to go to the grocery store. Here's a list of things we need."

He handed a piece of paper to Kimi, but she put her hands to her hips. "How come you get to do the fun stuff, and we're stuck with the groceries?"

Ben thought Wilson was going to crack a joke, but this was no time for playful jesting. "Sorry, girls. It's just that I know the guy who runs the bus company. I know he'll help us if I talk to him. Since Ben doesn't know his way around the stores, you'll be much more efficient at finding what we need. I'll come and help you carry the stuff as soon as I'm done, ok?"

Kimi's shoulders slackened, and she backed down. "Sure, Wil."

"Meet here in an hour," Wilson said.

They all nodded and headed off in different directions.

Ben felt a bit nervous at first, entering a hotel and addressing a dining room full of total strangers, but word of the stranded orca had already spread, and everyone was eager to take part in the action.

He headed out of a fourth inn, his spirits lifting at the thought of busloads of tourists coming to help. Now that the main road was practically cleared, maybe they'd even get a couple of bulldozers.

"Fancy running into you here," a voice said.

Ben whirled.

Jeremy Michaels stood behind him.

"You!" Ben gasped. Heat rose to his cheeks at the sight of the Provincial Times reporter. He tensed in unease. "Are you following me?"

Jeremy carried a hiker's backpack, wore brown walking boots and his camera hung strapped across his shoulder. He lifted his sunglasses, so they rested on top of his head and gave Ben a quizzical look. "Following you? Why would I be following you?"

Ben thrust up his chin in defiance.

Jeremy eyed him scornfully. "What? Am I not allowed to be here? I'm on assignment, kid. Haven't you heard? There's a whale beaching in the area. The Provincial Times sent me to write an article."

Ben did a double-take. He had not expected that. "You're lying! There's no way you could have heard about the beaching on the mainland. Electricity and phones are down."

Jeremy sighed heavily. "This is the twenty-first century, kid. There's long-range radios and ham radios and such. Besides, the mainland is always on alert when a storm hits the island, in case they need to send assistance or something. We found out about the beaching last night. I flew in at dawn."

As he spoke, Jeremy took a few steps forward, forcing Ben to step back. And suddenly he found himself in an empty side street.

He's trying to corner me!

Jeremy lowered his sunglasses over his eyes again. "Talking about lying, I could say a thing or two about the subject. You see, I've become quite familiar with Chilliwack. I've been talking to the locals there, asking questions about *The Cosmic Fall*. And I don't know why, but your name popped up, *Benjamin Archer*. Seems everybody knows the Archer family. They all know about the Archer boy who spent every summer vacation at his grandfather's house." He rolled his mouth to stress the words. "*Every*. Summer. Vacation."

He let the words hang, then said, "I became a reporter because I like to uncover the truth about things. So, you tell me, kid, who's the real liar here?"

He took off his sunglasses and glared straight at Ben. "Were you, or were you not, at your grandfather's house on August 26th, on the night of *The Cosmic Fall*? Did you, or did you not, witness the event?"

A shadow fell over Jeremy.

"Hey, you, why don't you pick on someone your own size?"

Jeremy spun around. "What the...?" he gaped, finding himself eye-to-eye with Wilson. The two were about the same size and age, though Wilson was muscled and tanned, whereas Jeremy was lanky and pale.

Giddy with relief, Ben ran to Wilson's side.

"I'm not picking on anybody." Jeremy protested. "What's wrong with you?"

"Come on," Wilson said, placing his hand on Ben's shoulder and leading him away.

Jeremy lifted his arms in resignation and shouted after them, "Hey, come on, you guys. I'm only trying to do my job."

Wilson walked away with quick strides, Ben jogging after him.

"Are you ok?" Wilson asked without slowing down.

Ben nodded wordlessly, glad to have the young man take charge without giving in to curiosity.

They found the girls by the pickup truck. Everything was already packed in the back: large hooks, strong ropes, buckets, towels, shovels... There were all kinds of things that could help them tow the orca back into the sea—things Ben would never have thought of.

"Get in!" Wilson ordered.

The girls exchanged a glance at his unusually bossy voice but got into the pickup truck anyway.

"Aren't we waiting for the buses to load?" Anna asked.

"There's no time," Wilson said. "The buses will come, eventually, but we need to go." His eyes met Ben's briefly.

Only Kimi caught the look. She stared at Ben, and he knew she knew something was wrong. She nudged him, but he only managed to give her a small smile in return.

He was not in the mood for talking. A reporter, who knew a lot more about *The Cosmic Fall* than he was comfortable with, was beginning to join the dots. He had tied Ben's name to the event.

That's not good. Not good at all...

But Ben's worries about his encounter with Jeremy Michaels soon vanished when they returned to the beach.

They found the neighbours hard at work, passing bucket after bucket of water from one to the other, splashing it over the killer whales. Ropes, lashed around the orca's tails, were pulled by small fishing boats in an attempt to slide the mammals back into the water.

But what hit Ben was the silence. The whales were no longer screaming in panic. Rather, their occasional cry reflected sorrowful resignation.

Ben and Kimi found Uncle Pete casting a grim look their way. He did not have any words of comfort for them.

The tourists arrived about an hour later—Jeremy Michaels among them—along with a dozen other Tofino inhabitants, and for a while, Ben's heart lifted. But by sunset, his hopes faded again.

Despite their best efforts, they only managed to free the baby orca and its mother. And although many killer whales were now half-way back into the water, it was not enough to lift them and release their six tons from the banks.

The weight of four cars...

Only professional cranes could have lifted such a mass. But they did not have cranes.

The tourists headed back into town, tired and sunburnt.

Ben watched helplessly as the locals slowly dwindled. He caught sight of Jeremy, who talked on his mobile phone while clicking away at his camera to catch the last rays of blood-red sun on the beach that would soon turn into a graveyard. They would make for a good headline story.

Worst of all was Kana'kwa's silence. Ben dreaded communicating with his new friend. Or rather, he dreaded the lack of communication, because Kana'kwa was unresponsive.

Ben listened to the orca's slow, booming heartbeat, wondering if there would be a next one and a next one...

"Ben!" Kimi came running up to him, her voice flustered.

He looked up at her, realizing he hadn't seen much of her all day. "What is it?"

Her lower lip trembled, and she glanced wordlessly down the beach.

Ben followed her gaze and saw a group of men in the dusk, walking up to the orca with determined strides. One of the men held a long, straight stick.

Not a stick.

A gun!

CHAPTER 12 *Negotiation*

Ben caught his breath at the sight of the gun and glanced, wide-eyed, at Kimi. She did not need to say anything. She already knew.

"No!" he gasped.

He broke into a run, Kimi following closely behind.

The man holding the gun turned out to be the local Sheriff. He stopped in front of the first beached orca and began to load the weapon, while another police officer left the group and combed the beach, shooing a couple of remaining bystanders away.

"Kid," the police officer barked as Ben ran straight towards him. "Get off the beach at once. This is no place for..."

Ben ignored him. He dodged the officer's reach and ran straight to the group of men, who alerted each other to his presence.

Uncle Pete detached himself from the group. "*Jongen!* What are you doing here? You should be home by now."

Ben landed in his grasp. "Uncle Pete, stop them!" he cried in panic. "You can't let them do this."

The five locals, among whom was the Sheriff, watched, their faces stern. The gun clicked as the Sheriff finished loading it.

"No!" Ben yelled, struggling to release himself from Uncle Pete's grip. "Please, this isn't right!"

"Pieter," the Sheriff said. "We can't have kids in the area. Send him home, or I will have someone take him."

But Uncle Pete gave him the tiniest nod, and the Sheriff lowered his gun. Uncle Pete turned to Ben. "Son, you were not supposed to see this." His face tensed, and he sighed. He took Ben more gently by the shoulders. "We have tried everything we could to get our friends back into the sea. But they are suffering. And we suffer with them. It is cruel to let the pain continue. This," he gestured to the gun, "is the only humane way to release them of their pain."

"No!" Ben shouted. "There has to be another way. More help is coming. There is still hope..."

Uncle Pete's empty eyes made tears well in Ben's own. "Please, Uncle Pete, give them another night. Just one more night." he begged, "There has to be another way." He shrugged Uncle Pete's hands off his shoulders and addressed the men. "Give them more time. Please!"

The Sheriff eyed him. "I'm sorry, kid. You're from the city. You don't understand these creatures' pain and suffering the way we do. I know this seems harsh to you, but this is the way we do things around here."

As the Sheriff finished, two men moved forward and grasped Ben's arms to pull him away. "No! Uncle Pete! Just one more night! Please! Give them one more night!"

"Hold it!" someone bellowed. "Leave the boy alone!"

They turned in unison, scanning the gloom.

"Pa, please!" the voice spoke again, and Wilson materialized from the tangle of dark bushes bordering the beach. He walked straight towards the Sheriff. "Pa," he greeted his father, slightly out of breath, then spoke to the Sheriff. "Sheriff Holmes. Forgive my intrusion." He glanced at Ben. "But, I respectfully ask you to listen to the boy."

Another form approached the group, and Ben saw it was Anna.

One of the men laughed. "Wilson, has love turned your brain into that of a jellyfish?"

Chuckles bounced around the group.

Even in the gloom, Ben saw Wilson blush. But it lightened the mood.

Sheriff Holmes addressed Wilson, "I remember when you were just a child, Wilson. You have returned a man with a voice worth listening to. But I will not let a city boy decide the fate of our killer whales. It is cruel to let them suffer any longer than they have to. The town council has decided."

"Then I ask the council to reconsider," Wilson cut in.

The men mumbled at his audacity.

Wilson glanced at Ben, then approached Uncle Pete and said in a low voice, "Pa, did you not say this boy was a *Dierenfluisteraar*?"

Uncle Pete blinked, clearly uncomfortable as he glanced at the other men to make sure they hadn't overheard Wilson. "Don't use that name in front of the others, Wil."

Wilson lowered his head. "I understand, Pa.

However, I stand by my words. I know for a fact that the boy is a *Dierenfluisteraar.* Didn't Kimimela's mother tell you something of the sort?"

Uncle Pete looked at his son, then at the men.

Wilson insisted. "Pa, I respectfully ask that you listen to the boy, and give the orca one more night."

The other men glanced at each other.

Uncle Pete sighed and nodded. He turned to the group of men and gathered them around him, whispering.

Ben forgot to breathe as he waited for their verdict.

Finally, the Sheriff turned to face him. "So be it," he said. "We will give the orca one more night." He pointed a finger at Ben. "I don't want to see you around here by dawn, boy. Is that understood?"

Ben gave a tense nod.

The Sheriff turned to leave, then added, "I will not sleep well tonight, knowing these poor creatures continue to suffer needlessly by your doing."

The men threw Ben a dissatisfied look, then headed back the way they had come.

Uncle Pete squeezed Ben's arm, then joined the group.

Ben felt his muscles weaken in relief, as he and Wilson watched the men leave.

"Well, there you have it, Ben-friend. One more night," Wilson said. "Though I really don't see what difference it will make. Even the tide did not pull the orca back into the sea. Only a miracle can do that now."

Anna approached and placed her hands on Ben's own. "I'm sorry, Ben," she said sadly.

Wilson put his arm around Anna's shoulders, and the couple walked away with their heads down.

Kimi came running to Ben's side, having been held back by the police officer combing the beach. She rubbed her hands over her pale cheeks. "What are we going to do now?"

Ben stared at the sea, the words that Wilson had spoken bouncing around in his mind. What was it that he had said? Goosebumps covered his arms. "The tide!" he breathed, adrenaline rushing through his body.

Kimi sniffled. "Yeah, that's what Wilson said. The tide came in while we were sleeping on the beach last night. But all it did was keep the killer whales wet enough so they could live another day."

Ben's eyes widened. His mouth fell open. *"The tide!"* He slapped his forehead with the palm of his hand. "How could I be so stupid?"

Kimi looked at him as if he had gone crazy.

A huge grin crept on to his face, excitement coursing through his blood. His voice trembled. "I know how to save the orca!"

The wheels in his brain turned at full speed like the engine of a locomotive. He glanced hurriedly up and down the empty beach. "A phone! I need a phone!" His eyes widened. "And I know just where to get one."

CHAPTER 13 *A call*

Jeremy Michaels crouched in his tent and connected his camera to his laptop so he could download his pictures. The laptop rested on his backpack, and the camera sat on a book on the ground. A camping light was swaying on a hook attached to the roof of the tent. To the side, the reporter had spread his sleeping bag and placed a neat pile of fresh clothes at the foot of it so he could change easily in the morning. His smartphone lay visible on top, so he wouldn't miss any incoming messages or calls.

He was still chewing at the last piece of caramel-and-nut bar, his fingers typing swiftly across the keyboard when a branch cracked outside.

"Who's there?" he yelled, all senses alert.

"It's me," a voice replied. "Ben Archer."

Jeremy stopped munching.

What's that kid up to now?

Jeremy unzipped the front of the tent, and a humid ocean air slapped him in the face. He stood protectively in front of the tent, allowing just a sliver of light to illuminate the kid. And beside him was a girl with long, black hair.

Great. Now there's two of them.

The kid gestured towards the girl and said, "This is my friend, Kimi. We're staying with her uncle and aunt not far from here."

Jeremy rested his weight on one leg, waiting.

The kid cleared his throat. "Um, I saw your tent," he said.

"So?"

"I also saw you using your smartphone on the beach earlier."

"So?"

"So, if you used your phone, it means communications are up again."

Jeremy crossed his arms in annoyance. "Get to the point, kid."

"I need to use your phone," the boy blurted, then added quickly, "Please?"

Jeremy's mouth opened in mock disbelief.

"Is that so? And may I ask why?"

"I need to call my mom. It's an emergency."

Jeremy snorted.

I knew he was up to no good.

"Um, let me see." Jeremy stared in the distance, pretending to think hard, then said, "No. Goodbye." He whirled and made to enter his tent again.

"Wait!"

Jeremy turned and looked at the kid again.

"Please, this is really important. It won't take more than a minute."

There was something about the kid's voice that almost made him give in. Almost. But then he came back to his senses. This was a boy he had come to mistrust. And he knew the feeling was mutual.

"Jeez'," Jeremy said. "Do you really think I'm going to lend you my phone just because you're homesick? That's my office phone, by the way. Do you know how hard I worked to get my boss to give me one of those?" He rolled his eyes. "What would you know?" He waved the kid away with his hand. "Go on, scram. Both of you. I've got an article to finish."

This time Jeremy entered the tent and zipped up the entrance, feeling a pang of guilt as he did so. He sat in front of his computer, his hands hovering over the keyboard. He was supposed to write but found himself listening instead.

Are they still there?

He couldn't hear anything. After ten minutes, he unzipped a corner of the entrance and peeked outside. Even in the dark, he could just make out the shore through the bushes and trees that protected his tent, but nothing else moved.

Some animal chirped nearby.

Jeremy shrugged, zipped up, and wiped his hands together.

Good riddance.

He settled down and raised his fingers over his keyboard again.

More chirping.

But this time, the sound came from close. *Very* close.

He froze, struck by a sudden certainty.

There's an animal in my tent!

Fear scurried up-and-down his spine. He whirled and found a tear in the fabric on the other side. Something rather large moved under his clothes.

"Aargh!" he shrieked, falling back in shock.

A raccoon popped its head out of his sweater, resembling a thief from a comic book. It stretched and eyed him curiously, it's pointy nose sniffing. Jeremy's smartphone wobbled in its dexterous paws.

"Oh no, you don't," Jeremy yelled.

The furry animal screeched.

Jeremy plunged after it, narrowly missing it as it slipped through the opening with his phone. "Come back here!" he bellowed.

Jumping up, the reporter bumped his head against the lamp, then stepped on his computer in his haste to get outside. Roaring, he tore at the zipper, rolled on the ground, and sprang to his feet like a ninja.

Jeremy scanned the darkness, a thousand nasty words racing through his mind. As the chirping receded, he balled his fists and hollered, *"Oh, you... you!"*

* * *

"Mesmo's in a meeting. Mom said she'll have him call right back," Ben said, thrusting Jeremy's phone on his sleeping bag.

"A meeting in the middle of the night?" Kimi raised an eyebrow. "I don't see what Mesmo could do. It's not like he can just beam himself over."

Ben hopped on one foot, then on the other, pretending to be cold. He walked over to his sleeping bag and lay down on it. "I just know he can help. There's nothing more we can do right now, except wait for him to get back to us." He zipped up the sleeping bag to indicate he wanted to get a shuteye.

Kimi curled up in her own sleeping bag, eyeing him silently.

Feeling awkward at not being able to give his friend more details, Ben placed Jeremy's phone next to him and cleared his throat. "Can I ask you something?"

"Mm." Kimi pulled the sleeping bag over her ears.

"Wil said something in Flemish to Uncle Pete earlier. He said I was a *zieflusterer*, or something like that. Any idea what it could mean?"

She didn't answer at first, and for a moment he thought she was tired and wanted to be left alone. Several times that day, she had seemed distant, as if something had bothered her. But then she turned on her back and blinked. "I don't know the Flemish word, but Wilson told me it means 'animal whisperer'. Wil and Uncle Pete's ancestors have known the ocean for so long that they have become one with the sea and the shore. They know the meaning of the ocean currents and the winds; they know which school of fish feed where, what they feed on, and which birds to follow for a good catch. The ocean is so ingrained in their lives that they've come to believe there isn't much difference between humans and sea creatures because they all form part of the natural world."

She turned to her side and closed her eyes. Her voice sounded muffled and drowsy. "Wil was telling Uncle Pete that you know something more about the sea than he does. It's not an easy thing for him to swallow. How could an outsider know more about the sea than he? But he trusts Wil, and so he trusts you."

She fell silent.

Ben sat with his arms around his knees, staring at the dark forms of the killer whales before him. A sprinkle of stars illuminated the crashing waves, and he thought of the immense world that lay beneath the water. A world he did not know that well but one which he had had a small glimpse of through the eyes of the creatures that inhabited it.

Humans were so busy on the surface of the planet. Why did they so ignore what lay below?

"Kimi?" he said.

There was no answer.

"Good night," he whispered.

She had given him an honest answer, but no more than that. Normally, they would have talked for hours, but it wasn't really surprising, he guessed, considering everything that was going on. It was best to let her sleep. Once this was over, he promised himself they'd talk more.

Ben yawned so hard his jaw hurt. His eyelids felt like lead. He settled further into his sleeping bag to fend off the chilly air.

It was his second night on the beach, and every muscle in his body hurt. He thought briefly of the comfy bed in Uncle Pete's house but quickly shut the idea out of his mind. As long as the orca were agonizing out here, he would stay by their side.

He glanced at Jeremy's phone. It was one o'clock in the morning. He bit his lip, feeling another wave of remorse at having stolen it, but this was a question of life and death. He'd return the phone by morning and make it up to Jeremy, somehow.

He snuck the phone into the back pocket of his jeans, then checked on Kimi, who lay fast asleep beside him, wondering once more if she was all right.

CHAPTER 14 *Tide*

"Benjamin?"

Someone shook him by the shoulders. Ben opened his eyes. He blinked and found Mesmo crouching beside him, his index finger over his lips to indicate silence.

Ben flung his arms around the alien, then checked on Kimi.

Boy and man got up and walked until they were out of earshot.

"Am I glad to see you!" Ben exclaimed.

"I came as soon as I could," Mesmo answered. "Your mom said it was urgent, that you were in some kind of trouble."

Ben shook his head. "No, not me," he said. "But them." He pointed at the orca, then took

Mesmo by the arm. "Come."

They approached the biggest orca, and Ben's hands glowed as he touched Kana'kwa's tough skin. The orca's pain made tears spring into his eyes. "This is Kana'kwa," he told Mesmo, then pointed at the other killer whales. "And this is her family. They are stranded and can't get back to the sea. We've tried everything, but have not been able to save them. Only you can do that, with your water skill." His belly fluttered. "What do you think? Could you do it?"

Mesmo glanced at the orca, frowning. "There are so many of them..." he began, then rubbed his chin, as if calculating his chances. "This is a job that would require at least three Toreq people skilled in water, but maybe..."

He paced up and down, analyzing the situation, then threw Ben a determined look. "I don't know, Benjamin. This is going to be hard, but I'll do my best."

Ben's heart leapt.

"Tell them to be ready," Mesmo said, then stepped straight into the waves, unfazed by the water's strength or temperature. His hands gleamed blue.

Breathless with excitement, Ben directed his thoughts to the killer whales.

Brace yourselves!

"Better move away," Mesmo yelled, before plunging his hands into the water. A blue glow seeped through the water from Mesmo's hands down the shore, reaching at least five orcas. The waves stilled as if listening to a silent command. Then the phosphorus liquid began rising up the beach, forcing Ben to step back further and further.

Ben could tell that Mesmo, who crouched with his hands outstretched, tensed under enormous concentration.

Orca vocalizations reverberated in the boy's mind, making goosebumps rise on his skin. Static filled the air, born from a fragile hope. Already, Ben could feel his body weight lighten as he rested his thoughts on the outskirts of the orca's minds.

The water rose, rose, almost covering the five whales' backs.

Mesmo's muscles trembled with the effort. He sustained the water with one hand and placed his other hand in the sand, forming an ice-sheet behind the whales. Then, just like that, he released his power. The air sucked at Ben's clothes, making him stagger forward. The water receded like a tsunami swallowed by a gigantic drain.

The orcas' clicks echoed across the beach.

Mesmo bent again, repeating the process, and each time, the killer whales slid back, some even rolling on their side, their tails splashing in the water.

This went on all night, five orcas at a time: Mesmo, crouching with his glowing hands in the sea, covering the mammals, then sucking the water, along with the killer whales, back into the sea. And Ben, running from one orca to the next, making sure they were free and unharmed.

The pod sang to one another anxiously, spouting fountains of water through their blowholes, and with painstaking effort, moved ever deeper into the bay.

By the time Mesmo and Ben were done, the beginning of dawn was creeping upon them.

The alien crashed on his back, gasping.

Ben crouched on all fours until he reached the alien's side. His body was so exhausted and exhilarated at the same time, that he couldn't stop giggling stupidly.

Mesmo stared at him and grinned.

"Lift your hand," Ben said.

Mesmo did so, and Ben slapped it hard.

"Ouch!" the alien said, glaring at him. "What did you do that for?"

Ben laughed. "That's a high five, dude! It's a

congratulatory gesture. Get used to it!" He rolled on his stomach. "We make a good team, you and I. If only the Toreq would work with humans. Together, we could make miracles."

Mesmo stared at the starry sky and sighed. "If only the Wise Ones heeded your words, Benjamin."

Ben lifted his head. "It's that bad, then?"

Mesmo nodded glumly. "I'm going to have a hard time convincing them to help us, Benjamin. When the Toreq banished the A'hmun to Earth, seven Wise Ones were selected among your people, the rare ones whom the Toreq still considered worthy.

"The Wise Ones were appointed custodians and ordered to report back to the Toreq on the doings of your species, with the promise of a one-way ticket back to the Mother Planet at the end of their lives, as thanks for their lifelong service. The Wise Ones have been abiding by this order for millennia, passing on their knowledge from one generation to the next. Changing their habits now will be close to impossible."

Ben lowered his head. "I'm sorry."

Mesmo stood and shook off the sand from his trousers.

Ben followed. "Don't worry," he said. "We'll

get them to change their minds. I don't know how yet, but we will."

Mesmo smiled. "Of course, we will, Benjamin. But right now, I have to get back. The last Wise One has just arrived, and I will begin the meeting. They will be wondering where I am. Plus, I wouldn't want anyone to stumble on the spaceship." He gestured towards the dense vegetation bordering the beach. He cast his eyes on Ben. "What about you? Will you be all right?"

"Yup. More than fine, considering everything that's happened."

Mesmo raised an eyebrow. "Really?" He smiled. "Then your mother was right. She *does* know you well. I was afraid you would hate us for sending you here."

They walked up the beach, Mesmo's arm around Ben's shoulders, his arm around the man's waist.

Ben shrugged. "It's just that, it's actually not that bad."

"Well, all right then. But remember one thing."

"What's that?"

"Stay out of trouble, ok?"

* * *

After saying their goodbyes, Ben ran back to the edge of the shore. The sky had turned a lighter colour. Some stars still clung to the night, but the bright rays of the sun began chasing them away from beyond the horizon.

It felt strange to see the empty beach, after having spent so much time with the orcas.

Ben scanned the bay and noticed many of the killer whales still lingered close to shore. They didn't seem in a hurry to leave. He guessed they needed time to recover from their ordeal.

It won't do to have them wash up on the beach again.

Remembering the small pier from which he had sailed with Wilson not long ago, Ben jogged down the shore and was relieved to find Uncle Pete's motorboat still attached there.

He hopped on and felt his way around the steering wheel, where he had seen Wilson hide the key. And lo-and-behold, there it was, stuck under a loose board.

The motor roared to life and Ben headed into the bay, approaching Kana'kwa. The voice that greeted him did not have its former strength, but it was not frail, either.

Benjamin Archer.

Are you all right?

Kana'kwa huffed through her blowhole.

We are tired, we are in pain, but we are alive. Thanks to you.

Ben grinned.

Yes, Kana'kwa, you will be alright. Just take it easy, and make sure you don't head towards the shore again.

Benjamin Archer, will you lead us? We are too tired and confused.

Of course, Kana'kwa. Tell your pod to follow me.

He took off again, heading the way Wilson had gone last time because it was the deepest and safest route.

Behind him, the sun rose, bright and warm, following the shiny backs of the whales as they breached and dove after the motorboat. Ben listened to the songs and clicks of the pod, as they communicated with each other. A mingle of prudent relief and disbelief echoed between them. And as the sea became deeper and deeper, a sense of exhilaration spread among them.

With each passing minute, the orcas had more space to dive, their aching bodies began to respond better, and for the first time since their beaching, they realized that they were going to live. They were free!

Their contagious excitement surged through Ben's mind. He thrust his fist in the air and whooped at the top of his voice.

Kana'kwa breached playfully and splashed a bucketload of ice-cold water over him.

Ben laughed and howled triumphantly.

Then, realizing that the open ocean lay not too far off between a set of islands, he switched off the motor, expecting the orcas to swim away.

Kana'kwa hung back.

Go on, Kana'kwa. The ocean is right before you.

Kana'kwa hesitated.

What's the matter?

It is the sea monster. It frightens us.

A chill ran down Ben's spine.

The sea monster...?

He didn't need to ask. Through Kana'kwa's senses, he heard the grinding sounds coming from the deep.

The pod hung back, hesitant.

It comes from behind that island.

Kana'kwa placed an image of an island topped with fir trees in Ben's mind. He turned his head towards the south and found the island.

He scanned it but saw nothing that could be

generating such a sound.

Then stay as far away from it as you can. Swim straight ahead, and you will be free.

A loud water-spout erupted from Kana'kwa's blowhole.

Yes, Benjamin Archer. We will head north, some distance from here. We will hunt for salmon there.

Kana'kwa's large head breached the surface, but close enough that Ben could touch it.

Goodbye, Benjamin Archer.

Goodbye, Kana'kwa. Be safe.

Ben watched as Kana'kwa headed after her pod, then sighed in satisfaction.

He was about to turn on the motor when something bright shone in his face. He shielded his eyes and searched for the source of the light. And then he saw it, behind the island that Kana'kwa had mentioned.

The bow of a very large boat.

It had been hidden before, but the tide had stretched its anchor chain until it became visible. Ben could just make out the letters on its side: SOVA.

Steel chains ground together and a deep thudding emanated from its hull.

Once more, an object on the boat reflected

the sun, causing a sharp light to flicker past Ben's eyes.

Suddenly feeling vulnerable on the water, Ben set his jaw and started the motor to head back to shore.

CHAPTER 15 *Rift*

Jeremy woke with a start, a headache hitting him like a hammer.

"Ouch!" he groaned.

He rubbed his temples, then realized several voices were coming from the beach.

He blinked and glanced around his messy tent. He had taped the torn fabric and had placed his backpack against it in the hopes that the sneaky raccoon would not return. The clean clothes he had extended on his sleeping bag lay in a heap in the corner. His computer remained unresponsive. Only his precious camera had come out of the night without a scratch.

Frustration surged in him again at the thought that he may never recover the orca photographs he had downloaded into his computer. And, without a phone, he had no way of contacting his office.

He had spent an hour stumbling around in the dark, searching for the damned raccoon and his phone.

Giving up at last, he had crashed on top of his sleeping bag, completely exhausted, and tumbled into a dream-filled sleep, haunted by strange, melancholic sounds and flashes of blue light.

From somewhere outside his tent, loud gasps and cries of joy drove his lingering fatigue away.

Intrigued, he picked up his camera, slipped his feet into his boots without tying the laces, and rushed to the beach, where he found an impressive gathering of people. An electric euphoria reigned in the air.

It took him a fraction of a second to realize why, and then, it hit him.

The orca!

His heart skipped a beat.

There wasn't a single killer whale left on the beach!

Were his eyes playing tricks on him? Yesterday, the beach was strewn with the massive black and white bodies of the sea creatures. Now, not a single one remained.

The orca had gone—vanished like ghosts.

For a second, his mouth fell open in wonder, then his reporting sense kicked in, and he rushed to the first group of people. "What happened? Where are the orca?"

Men and women turned to him with wide eyes, shaking their heads. "No one knows. They disappeared during the night."

"Must've been the tide," another one said.

Jeremy rushed past them, taking pictures of the gathering crowds, asking questions, and trying to find someone who had witnessed the miracle.

On the other end of the beach, a group of police officers and a girl with long black hair walked purposefully towards a small pier. Jeremy noticed they were heading towards a motorboat that was about to dock there. The boat was piloted by a single person. A person who looked strangely familiar... He zoomed in with his camera.

The kid!

He slowed down to a jog.

What was that kid doing on his own in the motorboat? If he had just come in from the bay, he must have been out there for quite some time.

Does he know what happened to the orca?

He clicked away with his camera, hurrying to catch up with the locals who surrounded Ben Archer as they headed off the pier and up the beach.

"Can I help you?"

Someone stepped in front of him, cutting off his path. It was that muscular guy with the tattoo of a four-masted ship, the one who had protected the kid in the back alley. He crossed his arms over his chest and glared at Jeremy.

Jeremy groaned. "Hey, man," he protested. "Get off my back already! I need to know what happened here! This is incredible! The world needs to know!"

"The world doesn't want to know. The world is too busy with itself. Some things are best left alone, trust me." The guy lowered his arms and glowered at Jeremy. "Go find something else to write about." Then he walked away, leaving Jeremy gaping furiously after him.

When the guy was at a safe distance, Jeremy jogged onwards, but by now, the police officers, the girl, and the kid were too far away, so he decided to walk to the end of the pier and get some pictures of the beach and the motorboat.

Jeremy mulled over the boy.

What is it with that kid?

Why did Benjamin Archer keep popping up every time something unusual happened?

He aimed his camera, zooming in on the wet tracks left by the boy and his followers, then stared at the empty horizon, deep in thought.

He was about to leave when something shiny caught his eye in the motorboat. Frowning, he hopped on and reached for the object. His fingers curled around the familiar gadget.

My phone!

* * *

Uncle Pete squeezed Ben's shoulders. "Son! *Mijn jongen*[5]!" he exclaimed, breathless with wonder. "You saved the orcas! How did you do it?"

Ben swallowed. He didn't want to lie. But he couldn't tell the truth, either. "I didn't do anything, really..."

"Pa," Wilson gave Uncle Pete a warning look. "The *Dierenfluisteraars* work in mysterious ways. It is not our place to question them."

Uncle Pete's face beamed, the corner of his eyes creasing with laughter lines. "Indeed," he said. "Let us leave it at that." They walked towards

---

[5] *Mijn jongen* : Flemish for 'My son' or 'My boy.'

the group of men, among whom was the Sheriff.

"There's something I need to tell you," Ben said, eager to change the subject. "Something confused the orcas and beached them. I think I know what it was. When I was out there, I saw a ship hidden behind an island. It's called the SOVA. It was making a lot of noise."

Uncle Pete glanced at the Sheriff. "I see," he said.

Ben continued. "We should go to the SOVA and let them know that they are putting the local wildlife in danger."

Uncle Pete lifted an eyebrow but did not answer. The Sheriff glanced at the other police officers.

Ben stared at them. "You already know about it, don't you?"

The Sheriff nodded. "We do. Don't you worry yourself with this. Let us take care of it."

"But..."

"That's enough, Ben!" Uncle Pete's tone of voice startled Ben.

The man softened his stance. "You've done quite enough, son. And you should leave that ship alone."

Ben opened his mouth.

The Sheriff spoke before he could say

anything. "I will report it to the Coast Guard as soon as I head into Tofino tomorrow." He saluted by tapping on his hat, then walked away.

"Tomorrow?" Ben glanced at Uncle Pete.

"Yes, tomorrow." Uncle Pete confirmed. "You did good today, son. Leave it for now. I want you and Kimi to head home and get some rest." He turned and followed the group of men. Glancing back, he urged, "Go on."

Ben watched them retreat down the beach. He set his jaw and glanced at Kimi, wondering what she thought of all this.

To his surprise, she did not acknowledge him but turned and walked off.

"Hey!" he called, suddenly realizing she hadn't said a word ever since he had docked at the pier.

She walked faster.

"Kimi? What's wrong?"

Her shoulders shook. She glanced back, her face twisted in anger. She seemed so upset she could not speak.

"What is it?" he exclaimed, truly worried this time. "Tell me what's wrong!"

"You really don't know, do you?" she burst.

"Huh?"

She walked swiftly, her face flushed. "You

went without me!" she yelled.

Ben flinched. "I... what?"

She stopped and balled her fists. "You saved the orcas without me! I know it was you. You did something, and you didn't wake me. My mom said, 'Don't you question him, Kimimela, don't you bother him'. And I obeyed. I've been silent all this time, trying to respect your private little life. But after everything I've done for you, you could have at least shared that moment with me. I thought we were friends. Friends share with each other: you know all about me, about my parents. My family has opened their arms to you. But you, you're full of secrets, aren't you? It's always the same with you. And I've had enough." She whirled and stomped away, leaving Ben gaping.

He was so taken aback that it took him a moment to start walking again. He stayed at a safe distance behind her, at a loss as to what to say.

A tightness gripped the back of his throat, as it dawned on him what he had done. He'd been so focused on saving the orcas that he had left his best friend behind.

But wasn't that what he was supposed to do? Sure, Kimi knew there was something different about him and Mesmo, but not once had she questioned anything, not even to ask about the odd events that had happened in her home town of Canmore. And he had stupidly considered that she was ok with it, that she was ok not knowing.

How wrong I was!

All this time, heaps of questions must have been gnawing at her mind, and he hadn't offered an inkling of an explanation.

He realized now why she had seemed distant. He had used his alien skill in front of her, causing a bunch of silent questions to resurface.

"Kimi..." he began, his voice full of remorse, but he didn't know what to say next, and she didn't stop to listen.

He followed her gloomily down the beach with his hands stuffed in his front pockets, wondering how to mend his friendship without revealing too much.

When they reached the house, Kimi stomped up the stairs and closed her bedroom door with a bang.

Auntie Jen stared after her, then at Ben. "Is everything all right, dear?" she asked worriedly.

Ben's eyes stung. "Um, I'm not sure," he managed.

Auntie Jen hugged him. "I am very proud of you. You did a brave thing today. You are the talk of the town."

"Auntie Jen?" Ben's voice sounded muffled in her shoulder.

"Yes, Ben," she said as if already expecting his question.

"Did you know? About the orcas?"

She kept stroking his back as if needing some time to think about her answer, so he pulled away and looked at her. "When you told that story about Lady Moon and Humbelfin, did you know the orcas were coming?"

She squeezed his hands in her own and smiled. "Some stories have been told so many times, over thousands of years, from generation to generation, that one is tempted to think they must have a reason for being. Where does fiction end and reality begin? Is there really such a place as The Edge of the Ocean, where half-moon and sea creatures meet? Perhaps we will never know. Or perhaps you are here to find out."

She released him and glanced up the stairs. "Don't you worry about Kimi. Give her some space. Things will work out, you'll see."

Ben swallowed.

"Go on, get some rest," she said. "You must be exhausted."

He was.

No sooner had she spoken than an immense

weariness sank into his body. "I think I'm going to lie down for a while," he agreed. He barely made it into his room and onto his bed. But just before plunging into a deep, dreamless sleep, he vaguely noted that Auntie Jen had not answered his question at all.

CHAPTER 16 *Staying out of Trouble*

Mesmo stared at the seven assembled men and women. Early dawn left a chill in the air. A fire burned in the middle of their circle. The leaves of the maple tree barely moved, as if they did not want to interrupt the solemn mood.

Mesmo took a long, straight branch that lay by his side and snapped off a piece. He placed the stick in his cupped hands, closed his eyes and spoke in a whisper. He invoked the wisdom of his ancestors, asked for foresight as clear as the stars and patience as deep as the universe. He asked to borrow the guidance and insights of his father, in anticipation of the difficult debate he was about to have with the Wise Ones.

He then stood, placed the stick in the fire, watched as it caught flame, then returned to his place. He glanced at his neighbour, who happened to be Einar.

The Norseman had finally arrived the previous afternoon. He had barely greeted them with a nod, then taken his place in the circle without offering an explanation for his late arrival.

Mesmo passed him the rest of the branch but held on to it just long enough to force the Norseman to glance at him before releasing it.

Pinpricks of light from the fire danced in Einar's eyes before he turned his attention to the branch. He then completed the same ancient Toreq tradition which always accompanied the beginning of a meeting, and was meant to bring clarity and hope for a positive outcome.

"I understand your skepticism regarding this meeting of Wise Ones," Mesmo said when they had all completed the tradition. "It is unprecedented and unconventional. Yet, it is also vital."

He stared at the circle of men and women who sat on the ground around him, shaded by the branches of the maple tree. Amaru, Yakut, Wonomanga, Akeya, Kahalu, Einar, Su Tai. They had all come at his calling.

"I have told you my mind regarding the descendants of the A'hmun, who now call themselves *humans* and who have inhabited this tiny planet for countless generations, ever since my people banished them here. However, now that I have observed them and lived among them, I have come to better understand why, a long time ago, the Toreq and the A'hmun were once close allies. And yet, at some point, for some undefined reason, this powerful and beneficial relationship soured to the point of no return and led to the disastrous Great War of the Kins.

"The Toreq's hate and fear towards this species have lingered, for we only remember their faults and have forgotten their strengths. It came as a surprise to me, therefore, to discover that their resourcefulness often eclipses their flaws, given the right conditions.

"And, as such, I have decided that I could not, in all consciousness, vote for the radical eradication of the human race."

He lifted his hand before anyone could object. "I understand that some of you agree with me, while others do not, and I assure you I have immersed myself in your life-long studies of the species, and taken your opinions into account.

"Therefore, in spite of your overwhelmingly

negative evidence against humans, I have advised the Toreq Arch Council against their elimination. And I have even taken things one step further."

He glanced at them, bracing himself. "I have decided to consciously and purposefully aid humans in becoming a better version of themselves. And I have gathered you here to request your aid in achieving this goal."

* * *

When Ben opened his eyes, the room no longer had sunlight beaming into it, though the blue sky outside confirmed it was still day. He rubbed at his eyes and face, feeling lines on his cheek where a fold of the cushion had pressed against it in his sleep. He hurried downstairs, checking in on Kimi's empty room on the way, and found Auntie Jen busy in the kitchen.

"Feeling better?" she smiled at him.

"Yes, thanks Auntie Jen. Have you seen Kimi?"

"I have. She's out surfing. Been gone an hour or so."

"Thanks!" Ben said breathlessly, turning to rush out the door.

"Now hold on a minute, young man. You've

got to eat something. You can't go out on an empty stomach."

Ben's stomach grumbled automatically. He checked the time and saw it was three o'clock in the afternoon. He had slept the morning away.

He gulped down a glass of milk and chomped on a Belgian waffle, then took a couple of wrapped chocolate cookies with him up to his room, which he dumped on his bed so he could pull on his wetsuit. He bit his lip, swaying between his desire to mend things with Kimi but realizing he also needed to do something about the SOVA. When he was changed, he stood unmoving in the middle of the room, heart thumping in his chest.

I'll need to take care of both.

Determined, he took out a piece of paper and pen and wrote: *Gone to the SOVA.* He left the note on his cushion, picked up the cookies and clambered down the stairs. "See you later, Auntie Jen!" he yelled, rushing out the door.

Reaching the path, he stopped and backtracked. Leaving without a surfboard would look suspicious, so he grabbed one that was leaning against the side of the house and headed to the beach.

He followed the shoreline, squinting at the waves. Surfers had once more claimed the beach, and it took him a while to discern which one of them was Kimi, but none resembled her.

Ben hesitated. He would have liked to talk to her, explain things so she would understand what he needed to do next, but she was nowhere in sight.

Disappointed, he headed to the pier for the second time that day. He dropped the surfboard and hopped on to the motorboat.

"What took you so long?" Kimi said.

Ben gaped. Kimi sat at the bottom of the boat, wearing her wetsuit and untying knots on a fishing net. Her long, black hair was tied loosely in a bun on top of her head, and she glared at him through the long bangs draping her eyes.

"I... er..."

She stood and narrowed her eyes. "I know where you're going," she said. "And you're not going without me this time."

Ben stared at her, at a loss for words.

"Stop gaping already," she scolded. "It's decided. We're going to the SOVA, and we're going to give them a piece of our minds."

"But... how did you know?'

She rolled her eyes. "Even if you never tell me *anything*, I still know you better than you think. You decided to go to the SOVA the minute

Uncle Pete told you not to. And I'm going with you."

Ben sagged into the driver's seat and stared at his friend. His heart bulged at her loyalty, but he was also extremely worried. "I don't know..."

"Oh, stop it!" she snapped. "You don't have to do everything on your own, you know? We're in this together. Don't you realize that yet?"

"I...," he fidgeted. "It's just... I don't want to see you get hurt."

"Oh, so it's alright for you to face danger on your own, but I'm not allowed to decide what I want to do?" she said. "This is not your decision. I'm coming with you, and that's final." She plopped on the other seat and crossed her arms over her chest in defiance.

Ben felt his cheeks burn. He wanted more than anything to be with her, but the responsibility fell on his shoulders. He knew things she didn't, and that put her at a disadvantage. "Kimi, if I haven't told you anything, it's because I'm trying to protect you..."

She snorted and checked the time on her wristwatch.

"Um, ok," he said, feeling as if he were walking on egg-shells. "Look, I'd like nothing more than for you to come along, but just so you're aware, I'm going to get into heaps of trouble when I get back. You, on the other hand, still have a choice."

"...and you don't?" she retorted.

Ben pursed his lips, thinking of the orcas, then replied firmly, "No, I don't."

The determination in his voice must have surprised her because she looked at him, and her face softened. "Then, I don't either," she said. She placed her hand on top of his. "I'm coming, ok?"

Ben nodded slowly. "All right." He forced a smile. "Thanks." He meant it. It felt reassuring to have someone by his side. He creased his face in thought. "We have to plan carefully, though. Like, we need to make sure we have enough fuel..."

"Done," she cut in. She lifted a fuel tank. "I filled her up and got some spare fuel, just in case."

Ben's eyes widened at her foresight. "O-o-k! That's what I'm talking about! And I left a message in Wil's room, so he knows where we are."

Kimi grinned at him for the first time. "Good. We'd better hurry, then, before Wil finds out."

Ben grinned back and started the motor. "We won't be long, anyway," he said.

CHAPTER 17 *The SOVA*

It took them a little over an hour to reach the SOVA. Metallic sounds from machinery somewhere inside the ship reached Ben and Kimi's ears, but in spite of that, the boat had an eerie and abandoned feeling to it, maybe because the black hull with yellow bordering its deck-line was smudged with corrosion and dents.

Ben navigated to its side, making sure the SOVA would not drift into the motorboat, even though it was safely anchored in deeper waters. Floating next to its imposing hull felt a lot more dramatic than Ben had expected. He tried to ignore his nervousness at the idea that he was about to communicate with the sailors on board. His nightmare clang to his mind.

Black owl, yellow eyes...

He exchanged a glance with Kimi, who nodded once in encouragement. He held his breath, feeling like a cheeky kid who had been challenged to knock on the grumpy neighbour's door, then run away before anyone could open it. He raised his fist and thumped against the hull, the thuds echoing deep into the ship's belly.

He took a step back and craned his neck.

Nothing happened.

"Try again," Kimi breathed.

He did, this time using both hands. He thumped as hard as he could. "Hey!" he shouted. "Hello, up there. I need to talk to you."

Kimi joined in. "HEEEY!"

They shouted and waved their arms. Ben pushed the side of the hull so the motorboat could drift back a bit. This gave them a better view of the deck way up above them.

Nothing moved.

"HELLO! HEY! Look down here!"

They yelled and yelled, but nothing happened.

Ben plopped in the motorboat, wondering what to do next. Could the crew have travelled to land for the day?

But then, his ears picked up the sound of

men's voices from the port side, and two heads popped over the railing. The men continued to chat together, even though they had spotted Ben and Kimi.

"Hey!" Ben shouted. "I need to talk to your captain. Can you call your captain, please?"

The pair continued to talk in a foreign language, ignoring him. Ben's heart sank. How was he going to communicate with them if they could not understand each other? He kept meaning to ask Mesmo. Why was it he could use his skill to communicate with animals, but not with humans?

The sailors disappeared.

"Oh, come on!" Ben said with annoyance.

Kimi stood beside him, her hands on her hips.

They yelled for attention again. Then a third man appeared and gazed down at them. He wore a sailor's cap and had a stubble beard. A cigarette hung loosely between his oil-stained fingers. He leaned over the side, resting his weight on his arms, then tapped at the cigarette, releasing ash from it.

Ben wrinkled his nose and brushed at the dust that landed on his shoulder.

The man took a deep inhale of the cigarette, then flicked the stump with the tips of his fingers, making the cigarette land in the water with a tiny fizz.

Now there were three men on deck, commenting and chuckling together. They did not seem interested in the teenagers at all.

Ben's cheeks heated with indignity. "HEY! YOU! I'm talking to you. Pay attention for a minute."

The man with the cap blew smoke through his mouth. "Vhat you vant, kid?" His deep voice bore a thick accent.

"Are you the captain?"

The man shrugged. "Vhat if am I?"

Ben's nostrils flared. "You need to listen!" he persisted. "We've come from the shore, where a family of killer whales got stuck on the beach. Your machines disoriented them. They managed to free themselves, but this could happen again. You need to move further away from the coast."

The man turned to the other two sailors, and Ben guessed he was translating what he had said.

Guffaws followed.

"Hey!" Ben yelled, his neck tensing. "What's the matter with you? Do you not understand what I'm saying? You're putting local wildlife in danger. You need to head back to the ocean."

The two sailors disappeared as if they'd

become bored by the show, while the smoking man propped his arms on the railing again and lit a new cigarette. "I indrested in zis vhale bizness. You tell more to me." He waved Ben to the centre of the ship, where metal rungs stuck to the side of the hull. "You come. Tell me of vhales."

Ben's lips tightened into a thin line as he considered the offer.

"Ben!" Kimi's warning whisper stopped him.

He glanced at her and saw her shake her head. *Don't do it*, she was saying.

Ben exhaled.

She's right.

His mom's voice echoed in his mind. "Never accept a lift from strangers," she'd say.

But I can't let them get away with this.

Ben ignored the fluttering feeling in his stomach. He approached the wheel of the motorboat, then glared up at the man. "There's nothing else to explain," he said, shooting him a fiery look. "We came to warn you about the damage you're doing and will continue to do if you don't go away now. The Coast Guard is aware of you being here, so consider this a friendly warning."

Ben turned the key in the ignition. The motor roared to life. He veered the boat slowly away from the hull of the SOVA, never taking his eyes off the man with the cigarette.

The man straightened with a smirk.

"Ben, watch out!"

Kimi's scream made Ben jump. He snapped his head forward.

From the bow of the SOVA, an inflatable dinghy emerged, roaring towards them at full speed, its outboard engine cutting through the water.

Ben's mind froze for a second before he realized the two sailors must have dropped it into the water *on the other side* of the ship so as not to alert him. He swung at the wheel of the motorboat, barely avoiding a head-on collision.

In a swift movement, the dinghy cut off Ben's path, and as soon as the two boats thudded against each other, one of the SOVA sailors hopped on board. He grabbed Ben roughly by the arm and shoved him aside, making him fall heavily on his back. The burly man twisted the key out of the ignition and cast the keys into the water.

"No!" Ben yelled, springing to his feet in panic, but another sailor reached for his shoulder from behind and pulled him into the dinghy.

Kimi yelled as the burly sailor dragged her

on to the dinghy, as well.

The second sailor grabbed a thick axe, jumped on to Wilson's boat, and hacked away at its bottom. The motorboat began taking on water, with Ben and Kimi watching in horror.

The burly man towered before them. "You. Up. Zpeak to gaptain," he ordered, pointing at the rungs of the SOVA.

Head spinning, Ben glanced helplessly at Kimi. His legs feeling like jelly, he stood and clambered up to the deck of the ship.

* * *

Mesmo watched the Wise Ones argue back and forth with tired eyes.

Ever since he had laid out the purpose of the meeting, asking them to help humans mend nature's broken balance, he had remained silent, letting the seven men and women debate whether this was allowed, conceivable, or even worthy of consideration. He had known it would not be easy. Finding common ground was going to be an almost impossible feat.

Einar did not speak, he noticed, and he worried deeply what the Norseman could be thinking.

"Mesmo," Wonomanga said in a warning voice. "Someone is here."

Silence fell over the group as they turned to watch a person walk towards them on the path by the cornfields.

Mesmo stood as a man in a grey business suit approached. They shook hands, and Mesmo said, "Thank you for coming on such short notice."

"I came as soon as I could," the man answered.

"Observer," Kahalu burst out. "Who is this? Explain yourself?"

Mesmo turned to the Wise Ones and said, "This is High Inspector James Hao from the Canadian Security Intelligence Service. He is the human expert on *The Cosmic Fall* and my trusted ally in my new mission to avoid a future confrontation with the Toreq. I have asked him to join us, so you can judge the seriousness of my resolve to help humans.

"The High Inspector has pledged to be a link between the human leaders and me, and I would wish for you to trust him in the same way."

Indignant eyes turned Mesmo's way as if the alien had broken a thousand unspoken rules in one go.

"Thank you for allowing me to take part in this meeting," Hao said, ignoring the cold stares. "A very limited group of people of the highest rank are aware of the Toreq threat. The government wishes to keep it that way until Mesmo, and—*ahem*—perhaps you, would be willing to reveal more. Several heads of state have been notified and have been given access to the remaining alien spaceship debris recovered from the crash site. As you can imagine, this event is considered a major threat to them, but I believe, with your help and insight, we could turn this to everyone's favour, for humans and Toreq alike."

Einar spoke for the first time, never taking his eyes off Mesmo. "Well, Observer, it seems you are many steps ahead of us. You bring forth this High Inspector without our prior approval, yet are you not conveniently avoiding the mention of another key negotiator in your elaborate plan? A human boy, who, I have heard, now possesses the Toreq translation skill."

All eyes were on the Norseman.

Einar continued, "Why do you bring forth this Inspector, yet, you do not bring forth this boy?"

* * *

Ben stood before the smoking man, whose cigarette hung precariously from the corner of his mouth. The captain sucked at the stub, then exhaled a cloud of smoke into Ben's face.

Ben coughed raucously.

The man waited for him to stop, then said with a smug look, "I Ivan, SOVA Captain. Vhen Ivan say, 'you tell of vhales,' then you come and tell Ivan of vhales. Time is money, *da*[6]?"

He tapped at a pair of binoculars that hung from his neck. "I make deal vhiz you. I vatch you zis morning. Vhales follow you. You tell Ivan vhere vhales go, then ve catch vhales. Customer buy vhale for vhale show. You make good money. You get rich."

Ben's legs went weak. He gaped at the captain. His mind reeled with worry, not only for himself and Kimi but also for the orcas. All he could manage was a shake of the head.

No way!

The captain pulled at the suspenders of his faded red fishing waders, then nudged his head at the sailors standing behind Ben.

They grabbed Kimi and led her to the

---

[6] *Da* = Russian word meaning 'yes'.

railing. She shrieked and fought back, but was no match for them.

"No! Wait! What are you doing?" Ben yelled.

The captain stepped forward and put his face inches from Ben's own, his small eyes hard as steel. "No deal, no girlvriend. You tell Ivan vhere vhales go, or girlvriend..." he made a slitting movement under his throat.

Ben's pulse raced in terror. Things were getting out of hand way too fast.

There was a pause, which lasted a fraction of a second, as they waited for Ben to react, but his mind had frozen.

Kimi cried out again, as the sailors made to throw her overboard.

"Ok! I'll tell you!" Ben shouted. "Let her go, please!"

The sailors loosened their grip on Kimi. She slipped out of their grasp and ran to Ben's side, sobbing into his shoulder.

"They went south, ok?" Ben said defiantly. It was all he could do not to burst into tears. "They went south."

The captain regarded him with emotionless eyes, puffing at his cigarette as if trying to decide whether Ben was telling the truth. Then he nodded slowly. "See? Deal not hard. But not good cooperation, so I keep vhale money."

Ben stood his ground. "I told you what you wanted, now let us go."

The captain smirked. "Ts, ts. Deal done vhen Ivan get vhales. Until then, you guests on great SOVA." His laugh chilled Ben to the bone.

"You won't get away with this. You'll have the Coast Guard all over your trail."

The captain eyed Ben from the corner of his eye. "Coast Guard?" He shielded his eyes with his hand and gazed at the empty horizon. "Vhere Coast Guard? Vhy small kids to come, and not mighty Coast Guard?" He pointed a finger at Ben's nose. "No, Ivan zink you lie. Zere is no Coast Guard." He turned and shouted gleefully, "Now, let's catch zome vhales!"

Ben's heart sank to the bottom of his feet.

The two sailors chuckled as they led the teenagers to the back of the ship.

Through stunned eyes, Ben watched as they marched along the trawl deck and passed a giant gantry crane, which stuck out from the centre of the ship. Then they followed a massive basin, which, he realized, was big enough to contain a killer whale or two. But there was no time to think about this because they reached a small stack of containers, one of which turned out to be empty and reeking of fish.

The sailors pushed them inside and shut the hinged door on them with a heart-stopping bang.

CHAPTER 18 *Precious Cargo*

Ben wrapped his arm around Kimi's shoulder and waited until she stopped sniffling. They sat to the side of the container, resting their backs on the hard, corrugated metal.

Rays of light from a couple of tiny holes in the roof hit the bottom of the container like laser beams, and Ben watched dust float around inside them.

He concentrated on not giving in to devastating panic at what he had done.

I shouldn't have brought Kimi.

His mind screamed with guilt. He should have insisted she stay on shore, even if it meant losing her friendship.

I should have known better.

He swallowed the painful lump in his throat. He'd have to get her out. He didn't know how, but that would have to be his priority above all else. And he'd have to think of something fast before the captain realized he had lied.

Because, of course, the orcas had gone north, not south.

* * *

Ben couldn't sleep a wink. Long, dark hours passed, and the temperature in the container dropped. He tried to avoid shivering in his wetsuit so as not to wake Kimi whose head rested on his shoulder, but every time his eyelids closed, he jerked awake again, heart thumping. What was the captain going to do when he realized Ben had lied about the location of the orcas?

Concentrate!

He needed to find a way out, come up with a strategy, a plan. Instead, he dozed off. If he hadn't, he would've known. He would've sensed them, the orca.

The door hinges squealed. The side of the container flung open, waking Ben and Kimi with a start. The two sailors appeared, their shapes cut out against the light of dawn. They barked at the teenagers and shoved them to the front of the ship in a hurry.

Ben couldn't think straight. His brain rang with exhaustion.

Pay attention!

Something was up, he could tell. But his ears wouldn't stop ringing. Overcome by a sudden sense of impending doom, Ben glanced down at his glowing hands.

...what?

He crossed his arms and stuffed his hands under his armpits in a hurry, feverishly trying to control the skill.

Kimi threw him a sideways look, eyes widening in alarm.

Captain Ivan stood waiting for them in the same red waders. He tugged at his cigarette, puffed a smoke ring out of his mouth, then crushed the stump under his thick boot.

His eyes narrowed as Ben approached. "You no good negotiator. You lie about Coast Guard to Ivan." He tapped his forehead with his index finger. "But Ivan smart. So, Ivan think: you maybe lie about vhales, too?" A satisfied grin full of blackened teeth spread on his face. "So, Ivan go north..."

Blood rushed through Ben's ears. He could

hear the orcas, even before the captain stopped speaking. Two of them broke the surface beside the SOVA, spewing air through their blowholes.

The captain's voice came from somewhere far away. "Ve hunt some vhales now, *da*?"

Something woke within Ben. Maybe it came from an adrenaline rush, or maybe from a feeling of helpless anger, but every cell in his body woke to the alien skill. He could feel it raging, like fire coursing through dry grass.

He was Ben, a boy standing on a ship, but he was also Kana'kwa, and Kana'kwa's daughter, and her grandson, and her uncle, and his son... He was the whole orca pod. He was deep in the ocean, in the midst of them, sharing their bond.

His human ears heard the gantry crane turn to cast its vast net into the ocean, while his heart thumped in unison with Kana'kwa's. And his word of warning exploded like a fireball through the ocean, booming, far and wide, like thunder crashing:

DIIIVE!

He felt the orca reel in response. They let themselves drop, far, far below the surface, their vocalizations crackling back and forth like lightning.

The net splashed, harmless, into the sea.

Head for the islands! Ben ordered, hoping they would find some protection there.

He followed the black and white shadows in his mind's eye, as they faded into the depth. His heart slowed considerably. The danger abated. He inhaled, long and hard.

The early sun shone bright white; the ship creaked as it moved to and fro, a warm breeze caressed his face, and around him, people gaped.

Kimi lay on the ground, staring at him. The captain hung on to the railing for dear life, eyes popping out of his head. The two sailors stuck to the wall as if flicked aside by a tornado.

Uh-oh...

Ben stared down and found that not only his hands but *his whole body* shone in a bluish light. Static ran up and down his spine as his cells absorbed the skill again. His skin prickled.

Jeepers! What have I done? What did they see?

The captain straightened, a mixture of fear and awe reflected in his eyes. "Vhat is zis?" he breathed. "Vhat are you?"

Ben's breath quickened.

One of the sailors spoke from behind. He was leaning over the side, and Ben guessed he had noticed the orcas were gone.

The captain barely glanced at the empty sea, then bore his eyes into Ben again. Fear seemed to win over his emotions, and for a split second, Ben was convinced the man was going to throw him overboard. "You not normal. You a vreak, a monster..." The captain wiped beads of sweat off his forehead. "...but valuable vreak. No vhales, but maybe zometing better, like vhale trainer..."

Ben could almost see the wheels in the man's brain spinning around.

The captain and the sailors exchanged some harsh-sounding words with each other, clearly undecided as to what to do next.

Kimi got herself off the ground, eyes glued on Ben.

Ben wished the skill would absorb quicker. He didn't like her gawking at him like that.

The captain clearly had the last say. He barked an order. The two burly sailors glanced at each other, uncertain, then stepped towards Ben.

"Leave him alone!" Kimi shouted, throwing herself at them.

But one of the sailors grabbed her wrist and held her at arms-length like a ragged doll.

The other one did the same with Ben, though at first, he hesitated.

But the captain spurred the ashen-faced

men into action, and Ben and Kimi found themselves heading back to their container prison.

As soon as the door shut on them again, Kimi kicked with her fists and feet against it. "Let us out!" she shouted, over and over.

Ben stood behind her, his heart heavy, and waited until she had exhausted her frustration.

Finally, she stopped and hung her head.

"Kimi?" he said, testing his voice to make sure it wasn't trembling too much.

She didn't move. "Yeah?" Her voice sounded muffled.

"Maybe I should tell you now."

She turned to face him, eyeing his glowing hands warily. "Tell me what?"

He caught his breath, then said, "Everything."

She stood like a statue.

He guessed she was waiting, so he began to talk.

She didn't say a word. She didn't even react when he explained the most unbelievable details of his adventures. He told her about *The Cosmic Fall*, about his alien skill, and even about The Great War of the Kins. He had no idea whether she believed him or not and didn't have the energy to worry about it at this point. Perhaps she would never want anything to do with him again, but he would have to accept that. She had the right to know and then decide what to do next based upon that knowledge.

When he was done, she stared at him for a long time.

By now, they were sitting, cross-legged, facing each other.

Finally, she said, "I guess you were right."

"About what?" he asked, confused.

She sighed. "About getting into trouble."

He bit his lip. "I wasn't expecting this much trouble."

She fell silent.

"I'm sorry," he added weakly.

She nodded.

He waited.

"I don't know what to think, right now," she said in a tired voice.

"That's ok. You don't have to think anything. Just let it sink in."

Her chin trembled. "Ben?"

"Yeah?"

"What are we going to do now?"

His shoulders drooped. "I don't know."

CHAPTER 19 *The Hold*

The sailors brought them some blankets and soup.

Ben and Kimi weren't hungry, but they figured they should eat to keep up their energy. They stared at the greenish slush, wondering if it was safe to eat.

"Let me test it, first," Kimi said. "Just in case."

Before Ben could say anything, she took a spoonful. He opened his mouth to scold her, but it was too late; she had already swallowed. They stared at each other, then she said, "It's yucky, but there's nothing wrong with it."

Ben forced himself to swallow a couple of spoonfuls, but his stomach twisted with worry, so he shoved the bowl aside and lay down.

Kimi did the same, though not too close to

him, he noted. He wondered whether she would ever trust him again.

They remained like that in silence, until Ben figured Kimi had fallen asleep. Or maybe she was only pretending, so they wouldn't need to talk.

He felt his eyes prickle with fresh tears, but then heard her turn to him and say, "Ben?"

"Uh-huh?"

She fell silent for a moment, then said, "Thank you for telling me."

He smiled in the gloom.

She paused again, then added, "You know I believe you, right?"

His smile widened. He swallowed the lump in his throat. "Thanks," was all he could manage. Maybe she was just saying that to be nice, but it lifted a weight off his shoulders anyway. He closed his eyes and fell fast asleep before he could stop himself.

* * *

The door hinge creaked.

Ben's eyes shot open.

What now?

He leapt up, Kimi by his side. She grabbed his arm as the door opened a crack.

The shadow of a man emerged in the entrance, revealing a drizzle in the dusk outside.

No one moved.

"Well, don't just stand there! Hurry up! I haven't got all day," the man said, waving a flashlight at them.

Ben and Kimi squinted. This was not the usual sailor. But that voice...

I know that voice...

The man sighed in annoyance. The door opened wider. "Are you coming or what?" He turned the flashlight, shining it on his face.

Ben gasped. "Jeremy?"

"Yes, Jeremy. Provincial Times. Remember?"

Ben's eyes widened in shock. "What are you doing here?"

"What does it look like I'm doing?" the reporter snapped. "Saving you, is what I'm doing. And risking my neck while I'm at it."

Kimi whooped.

"Shhhh!" Jeremy said urgently.

Kimi rushed forward, but Ben held her back. "Wait a minute. If this is a ruse to get us into one of your breaking news stories, we're not interested..."

"Use *you* for a story?" Jeremy scoffed. "A simple 'thank you' would've been nice. What the heck were you thinking, confronting this ship's crew on your own?"

"That's none..."

Kimi cut in. "Hey, boys! Can we talk about this later?"

Ben's face flushed. He set his jaw and spoke to Jeremy. "She's right. I'm sorry. You lead the way."

Jeremy nodded darkly, moving aside to let them out of the container.

They crouched behind a heap of fishing nets, hunkering as cold raindrops slid down their faces and surveilled the deck.

Ben banged his knee against a bag that hung from the reporter's shoulder. *His camera...* "Seriously, what *are* you doing here, Jeremy?" he asked again.

Jeremy shot him a look. "You've got a thick skull, kid. You managed to steal my phone; you won't reveal how the orca got off the beach; then you head straight for a ship that reeks of illicit doings... You betcha bottom dollar I was going to follow you. I snuck on to the ship when I saw them grab you. I've been cramped in a closet for days. Couldn't get out because it turned out to be near the crew mess—you know, where sailors eat?"

A loud noise startled them into action. Some

kind of machinery had been set into motion.

The three of them sprinted towards a door and snuck inside. They found themselves in a narrow corridor, listening for any sounds indicating that the sailors had found out their prisoners had escaped. A constant grinding sound of metal coming from the belly of the ship sent a shiver down Ben's spine. It reminded him of his nightmare.

"Now what?" Kimi breathed.

Jeremy ran a hand through his curly hair. "Getting you out was my priority. The crew has been sailing full-speed all day. We're way out in the open ocean by now. We're going to have to find a place to lay low until we reach port."

Ben tensed like an arrow. "What? That could take days! They'll find us, for sure!" He slapped his forehead. "Wait a minute. How did you even get here? Swim?"

"No, I did not swim." Jeremy spoke slowly as if to contain his temper. "I had a motorboat, believe it or not, but when you got yourselves caught, I had no choice but to leave it behind."

That silenced Ben. He didn't know why he kept snapping at the reporter. He felt like he was releasing hours of piled-up fear, and poor Jeremy just happened to be on the receiving end of it. He took a good look at the pale reporter, noticing pearls of sweat on the man's forehead. Spending hours hiding in a closet clearly hadn't done him good.

This is all my fault, Ben reminded himself. Jeremy and Kimi were both in danger because of him. That thought made him focus. "Look, I'm sorry. I didn't mean to snap at you. I..."

A door opened somewhere down the corridor.

"Go, go, go!" Jeremy urged.

They ran the opposite way, descending stairs and turning corners. Jeremy opened a heavy door. They stepped inside in a hurry, only to be met with icy air. They stared at heaps of neatly packed fish stacked in crates before them.

"The freezer hold," Jeremy said, a cloud of cold mist forming before his face.

"What type of fish do you think these are?" Ben whispered, picking up a plastic wrapping and trying to decipher the label written in a foreign language.

"No idea," Jeremy said, grabbing his camera and taking quick pictures of the hold and its contents. He slipped his camera back into the bag, along with a well-sealed package. "Could be illegal fishing or even whale meat. I'm thinking we're on a small-scale factory ship."

"What's a factory ship?" Kimi asked as they snuck back the way they had come.

"It's a commercial ship that's large enough to catch, process and freeze large amounts of fish all in one go. The largest ships rake the ocean with nets that can reach two kilometres in circumference. It's estimated entire fish stocks will collapse worldwide before the end of the century if these things continue to operate."

Kimi gasped as she tried to keep up with the reporter's fast strides. "That's terrible!"

"Is it, really?" Jeremy said sarcastically, stopping before another door and eyeing her. "Where do you think your supermarket fish comes from?"

Ben glanced at Jeremy, surprised at the reporter's knowledge, and realized, for once, that perhaps they were not working in opposing directions. It suddenly dawned on him that this reporter's insights meant everything.

Jeremy pushed the door open, and this time, they found themselves in a processing room. They leaned on the railing and took in the cavernous area that could have fit an Olympic pool.

"This is where they would have transported

the killer whales," Kimi noted, reading Ben's mind.

"Killer whales?" Jeremy wiped at his brow, glancing her way. "You mean this has to do with the beached orca?"

She nodded. "The captain said they were trying to capture the orca for some kind of whale show. But the orca fled towards the beach and got stuck."

"A whale show? Ah, that would make sense. Once a killer whale is trained to entertain, its owners can make millions off of it."

"I thought those types of shows were illegal?"

"Some countries still allow them, or they simply turn a blind eye to the practice. I wonder why the crew gave up on their chase, though. Why would they leave empty-handed...?"

"Guys," Ben interrupted. "Do you hear that?"

They listened, bodies tense.

"I don't hear anything," Kimi said.

"That's because the ship has stopped!" Jeremy gasped.

Goosebumps rose on Ben's arms. The metallic hull pinged with static, and the ship swayed harder than before.

Kimi's eyes filled with panic. "Do you think they found out we escaped?"

Ben's stomach was still churning from imagining Kana'kwa stuck in this place. "No idea. Let's get out of this processing room. I don't like it." He pointed at a door with a red sign on top of it at a higher level.

I hope it says EXIT.

He passed by Jeremy, who clung to the railing.

"Are you ok?"

The reporter's face was grim, but he nodded and waved him on.

Ben climbed the metal stairs that bordered the pool. The hairs on the back of his neck prickled, probably because loud sounds of grating chains suddenly cut the silence. Reaching the landing, he peeked through a round window in the door. On the other side, he spotted the deck and ocean.

Bingo!

He tried to turn the lock wheel to open the door, but it wouldn't budge.

Jeremy pushed past him. "Hold this a minute." He handed Ben his waterproof bag, then groaned with effort as he pulled at the wheel.

"Hey, guys, I've got an idea!" Kimi said, coming up behind them. "I know how we can escape! We could use the ding-"

A blaring alarm drowned her words. Above them, the ceiling began to slide open. Ben gaped as the gantry from the center of the ship appeared. And from this tall crane, a massive, bulging net crammed with fish hung precariously above them.

"Got it!" Jeremy yelled, pulling open the door.

Kimi rushed after him.

But Ben forgot about running to safety. Millions of tiny voices crashed into his head from above, stunning him. The blood rushed through his ears, his hands glowed, and his mind swayed.

He caught his breath and pressed his eyes shut, just in time to control his thoughts. "Wait... I can't..." he gasped, reaching for the door, which clicked shut under his fingers. He glanced through the round window.

Jeremy lay sprawled on the deck, unconscious, heavy-set sailors looming over him in the pouring rain. One of them held a struggling Kimi in his grasp.

Just as the sailor turned his way, Ben slid down with his back against the door. He grabbed the lock wheel and turned it with all his might, shutting out the men.

And Kimi.

He crouched into a fetal position, pressed his hands against his ears, and braced himself as the net released the millions of fish into the basin below him.

CHAPTER 20 *A Risky Plunge*

"Ben?" Kimi called him from somewhere far away.

He could hear the fear in her voice as he struggled to regain consciousness.

"Ben!" she called again.

He blinked and found himself alone, lying on the metal passage he, Jeremy, and Kimi had used.

How long have I been out?

"Ben! Don't listen to them! You can escape!" Kimi's voice burst through a speaker that echoed into the vast basin room. "Don't lis-" The speaker whistled, making Ben covered his ears.

Silence followed.

I can escape?

His mind whirled. Quick! What had she been

trying to say before the ceiling opened? Something about a *ding*.

What's a ding?

He lowered his hands, standing on wobbly legs. He picked up Jeremy's waterproof bag, passing the strap over his neck and shoulder, then leaned over the railing to take in the contents of the basin below. Millions of silver fish lay sprawled within, motionless.

The speaker crackled, and the captain's voice reverberated against the walls like a mummy speaking from the entrails of a tomb. "Vreak boy. You listen now to Ivan, *da*?"

The pause that followed lasted long enough for Ben to realize he was breathing way too fast. He swallowed through his dry throat and listened.

"Ivan not in mood for SOVA search. Time is money. Customer vaiting. Ivan deliver chop-chop."

A strange whooshing sound came from the speaker, making Ben jump. But then he realized the captain must be smoking. He could picture the cigarette dangling from the man's lips.

"Vreak boy chase away vhales. Ivan lose business. So, Ivan make deal to deliver vreak boy instead. Train vhales, *da*?"

Ben shut his eyes, wishing he could unhear

203

the captain's words.

Come on, Kimi! What were you trying to say just now?

"Ivan give ten minutes to meet at back of ship. Ten minutes, or vriends vish vood..." He let the phrase hang. "You understand, vreak boy?" The speaker squeaked, then went dead.

Ben uncurled his hands, his knuckles white from having gripped the railing too hard.

Ten minutes!

He had ten minutes to save Kimi and Jeremy.

* * *

Finding the way back took Ben a full five minutes.

His heart raced at the rhythm of his hurried footsteps as he backtracked through the corridors and up to the next level. He spotted another door with an EXIT sign on it and opened it a crack.

Finding the coast clear, he stepped onto the deck once more. Cold wind whacked at his cheeks. Rain battered his hair and face. Lights flickered on around the ship. The SOVA rested on the dark ocean with its motors at a standstill.

Voices reached him. Searching left and right,

Ben found rungs which he used to heave himself onto a roof. He rolled flat on his stomach just in time as the captain and a sailor walked by below him. The captain stopped and blew a cloud of cigarette smoke that caught in Ben's nostrils. He stuffed his face into the cradle of his arm, fighting a sneeze.

When he looked up again, the men had moved away towards the back of the ship.

Ben straightened, fully conscious that he was out of options. He climbed down the rungs, shivering under the enormity of their failed escape. He was going to have to hand himself in.

He took a few steps forward.

That's when he saw it, suspended by ropes and hanging over the side of the ship.

The dinghy!

Of course! *'Ding'-hy...* That's what Kimi had meant! She wanted him to take the SOVA's inflatable dinghy and escape.

He caught his breath.

No way!

He couldn't leave Kimi and Jeremy to their fate, could he?

* * *

They were waiting for him by the railing at the back of the ship: the captain, a sailor, Kimi, and Jeremy. Jeremy sat on the floor, rubbing his head.

They hadn't seen him yet.

The captain checked his watch. "Is late," he observed, clenching his jaw, so that cigarette smoke escaped through the slit between his lips. He shoved Jeremy in the back with his boot. "Not good vriend, dis vreak boy?"

Ben crept up a set of metal stairs leading to a ramp overlooking the stern side, located just behind the gantry. Rain pelted his face. He puffed his cheeks. *Here goes nothing...*

He stepped under a bright neon light, casting a shadow below him.

The captain caught the movement and removed the red cigarette stub from his lips. Smoke billowed from his mouth into nothingness. "You late. Come down, now, vreak boy."

Ben shook his head in defiance. He had to gain some time.

Please, please, let this work!

The captain flicked the cigarette over his shoulder and into the black water behind him. "You not want to make Ivan go up zere," he threatened.

Ben stepped closer to the railing. "I'll come down. But first, let my friends go."

A look of fake surprise crossed the captain's face. "Go?" he asked, looking around him. "Go vhere?" He spoke to the sailor, who laughed loudly.

Ben stood his ground. "I mean it!" he yelled. All he needed was to give Kimi and Jeremy a bit of space. He focused on Kimi, holding her gaze as long as possible. Would she understand, when the time came? Would she trust him enough to do what needed to be done?

The captain shrugged, looking amused. "Vhatever." He gestured with his hand for Ben to come down.

The sailor let go of Kimi and Jeremy, who stepped away. The reporter clung to Kimi's shoulder, his face ashen.

This is too easy. Where's the second sailor?

As Ben stepped down to the deck and spotted him. The second sailor was climbing a parallel set of stairs leading up to the ramp. If Ben didn't hurry, he and his friends would be cornered. He had no choice but to walk towards the captain. Even if his plan didn't work, at least his friends would be out of these men's hands for a while.

He and Kimi crossed paths. She stared at him with wide eyes that said, *What are you doing?*

Out of the corner of his mouth, Ben whispered, "Jump!"

Her head snapped his way, eyes popping. Her mouth opened in silent disbelief, *Are you mad?*

Ben whirled, standing steadfast between the captain and his friends. *"DINGHY! GOOO!"*

Kimi blinked at him once. Things moved in a flash. She grabbed Jeremy by the arm and ran straight for the railing. Jeremy's eyes widened in terror. Then, in less than a heartbeat, both disappeared over the side.

The sailors dashed after the two fugitives, blocking Ben's escape. The captain lunged, his fingers wrapping around Ben's wrist. But the man slipped on the rain-soaked deck, bringing Ben down with him hard.

Ben slid out of the clasping fingers in the nick of time. He jumped to his feet and ran towards the containers. His feet splashed through rivulets of water as he dashed between them. He gasped.

Three against one.

They would catch him for sure. Ben's heart palpitated so hard he thought it would bounce out of his chest. He had to act now, or he'd miss the dinghy. He ran straight to the other side of the ship through pouring rain.

But one of the sailors had foreseen his move and was waiting for him by the railing. Behind him, the captain huffed as he barreled between the containers after him.

Trapped! Unless...

The ramp he'd been on a moment ago lay to his left. Desperate, Ben dashed up the steps, two at a time. He clambered over the railing at the top and peered at the dark, swirling waves below. His brain swayed at the height.

Too high!

Thudding footsteps approached behind him.

Way below, to Ben's right, Jeremy was pulling himself out of the sea into the dinghy while Kimi was unfastening the last rope that held it to the ship. She glanced up at him.

Ben shut his eyes and jumped.

CHAPTER 21 *The Pillars of the Sea*

Ben's body slammed into the ocean. It swallowed him into an oppressive silence. Freezing water seeped into his wetsuit. For a split second, he thought he was tumbling down the abyss at Motu Oné. Only, Mesmo wasn't there to catch him this time.

He thrust his arms around in a panic. His head popped out of the water as he caught the trough of a wave. He gulped in air just before the crest caught him and sent him under again.

A deafening rumble almost made his heart stop. Something dark passed near his head.

The SOVA!

Churning water from the ship's wake sent

him even deeper, almost making him succumb to terror.

Is this it, then?

He stopped thrashing, giving in to the weightlessness, listening to his heartbeat—the only sound left in the universe. His body slowed to a stop, suspended in the cold liquid as if it were suspended in space. His heart rate decreased, and as it did so, his thoughts cleared.

T-H-U-D.

His heart beat once, loud and slow. He felt the ocean current brush against his skin; a giant, invisible waterway in constant movement. He knew where it came from and where it went as if he had known it all his life.

His body drifted to the surface again, and he breached the waves in slow motion, taking in a fulfilling gulp of air this time. His eyes briefly took in the black night. His radar senses picked up the hard hull of the receding SOVA, a dinghy bobbing up and down not far off, the smell of land miles away. He could pinpoint its location with precision because he had travelled these waters year after year, generation after generation.

He closed his mouth and let himself sink again.

T-H-U-D.

His heart must surely be bigger than his entire body. His senses slowed almost to a stop, becoming ever more receptive and acutely aware.

The water wasn't that cold after all. The depths weren't that dark. Instead, he sensed the shape of the ocean bed below him: its chasms, mountains, valleys and creatures. Millions of creatures. Some big, some tiny. Some with sharp teeth, some without. Scaly, wiggly, soft-skinned, hard-skinned, hiding under shells or scampering across the seafloor. He knew them all because his kind had roamed these waters for millions of years.

He rested his mind on the ocean current that carried his thoughts many miles away, then swerved deep down to the Earth's bed. He travelled through a rift made from a colossal corridor of rock. Ghostly sounds bounced against its walls, brushing by him like invisible tentacles, and when he broke into a vast opening, he found the source of the creatures that had connected with him.

T-H-U-D.

The dark outline of five blue whales towered before him like giant pillars of the sea. They hovered, immobile, with their tails pointed down and their heads facing up to the distant surface like massive submarines, and though they seemed to be sleeping, Ben knew this was far from the case.

Their song reverberated far and wide through the ocean, amplified by the repetition of each others' vocalizations.

The biggest whale in the circle addressed him defiantly. *You should not be here.*

Ben cringed. *I don't understand. Then why are you showing yourselves to me?*

Because we were curious. No two-legged creature from the world beyond has spoken our tongue before.

Ben hovered in thought in the midst of them—a speck facing giants. While only the biggest blue whale addressed him, the others never ceased to cast their songs out into the ocean, as if they were sending a universally understood call. And, in response, Ben sensed many sea creatures approaching the circle.

What is this?

It is The Gathering...

No sooner had the biggest whale spoken, than one of the others spun on itself, its car-sized flipper causing a whirlpool around it, and let out a deep warning note to end the conversation.

In response, the biggest whale slowly broke

off the connection with Ben, as if it suddenly realized it had said too much.

But Ben wasn't ready. His mind spun.

An ocean gathering! That's exactly what I need!

For... for what? He couldn't remember. The whales' overpowering presence paralyzed him, and the memory came from another part of his brain that he was not connected with right now.

T-H-U-D.

His heart beat in unison with that of the five blue whales. He clung to the last mental threads connecting him to the biggest whale.

I must be at this gathering! There is something I need to tell you. It's important!

He'd have to figure out what it was, and quick!

The biggest whale reprimanded him:

You are not welcome here. You must return to the girl.

The girl? Ben's mind reeled. *What girl?*

He could see her: dark eyes, flowing black hair. He wished she would stop yelling at him; he couldn't concentrate.

The whale repeated: *You must return to her, or you will drown.*

Why would I drown?

The whale released his mind without answering.

T-H-U-D. Thud-thud, thud-thud...

Increased heartbeat. His senses reconnecting with his brain. Body screaming for air. Ben opened his mouth. Water cascaded into his throat. Burning!

Can't breathe!

Kimi screamed, "BEEEN! Please! I can't hold on much longer."

Ben vomited water. He coughed, wheezed, and coughed again.

She had his arm pinned to the side of the dinghy, hanging on to him for dear life. "You're too heavy!" she shouted.

Waves slapping his face. Legs flailing aimlessly below the sea. Ben blinked the drops from his eyes. He flung his free arm and hooked his hand to the side of the dinghy.

Kimi groaned as she strained to pull him on board.

He didn't have an ounce of energy left in him, yet he knew he must do something. He inched his way up and over the side, then landed heavily on the bottom.

"Are you *crazy*?" Kimi yelled, furious, as Ben struggled to a kneeling position. "Don't you *ever* do that to me again!"

The part of Ben's alien mind that still lingered below the waves connected sharply, and he realized with a jolt who he was and where he was. He took in the girl in the wetsuit and remembered...

I asked her to throw herself blindly into the middle of the ocean!

The realization made him woozy. What a cruel thing he had asked of her! She had almost drowned in a frozen lake not so long ago.

He shook his head, dumbstruck. "Never again. I promise."

She threw her arms around him and squeezed hard.

He glanced over her shoulder and took in the pinpoints of light from the SOVA through the drizzling rain.

"I'm sorry," he mumbled, horribly aware of the dangerous feat they had just accomplished in the dark.

If any of them had missed the dinghy...

"Do you think they'll come back?" Kimi asked.

Ben realized she, too, was looking at the receding SOVA. "I don't think so," he said, hoping he was right. "They'll never find us in the dark."

Ben caught his breath. "How did you find me, anyway?"

Kimi pulled back, her face pale, her eyes wide. "Are you *kidding* me right now?"

Ben blinked, then glanced down at his glowing body.

"You were like a lightbulb down there. I could see you for miles."

Ben brushed at his arms. "What's happening to me?" he whispered.

Kimi looked at him, pale-faced. "Are you ok?"

Ben thought about her question. "Actually, I feel great!"

Like a charged battery.

The thrill of communicating with the sea creatures still lingered in his mind. But this new phase in the alien skill also meant trouble. It was one thing to hide his glowing hands, but his whole body?

I need to have a word with Mesmo.

His skin prickled as his blood cells absorbed the skill again.

"You *are* crazy! You know that?" Kimi said with a nervous laugh.

Ben broke into a grin. "I know, right?" Then he remembered Jeremy and whirled. "Where's

Jeremy?" He hadn't heard the reporter since he had climbed aboard and now found him lying curled up in a ball at the front.

"I don't know what's wrong with him," Kimi said, eyebrows creasing. "He's only half-conscious."

Ben placed his hand on the young man's front, which felt cool enough. At least he wasn't running a fever.

Jeremy groaned and tried to open his eyes.

"Jeremy," Ben called anxiously. "What's the matter?"

The reporter moaned and flopped to his side. He opened his mouth to say something, then instead crawled hurriedly to the side of the dinghy and retched.

Kimi held on to the man's arms to sustain him and glanced at Ben with a quizzical look. "I think he's seasick," she mouthed.

Ben sat back, puffing air out of his cheeks.

Seasick!

Suffering from seasickness felt awful, no doubt, but at least it wasn't deadly.

Jeremy kept surprising him. Had he been seasick the whole time he had been on the SOVA? Ben felt a pang of guilt mingled with new respect towards the reporter. He was tired of getting everyone into trouble. It was time to put things right.

"Ben?" Kimi said, pulling him out of his thoughts. "I think we're ready to go home now."

CHAPTER 22 *The Gathering*

They didn't have enough fuel. Ben knew this for certain because the blue whale's lingering thoughts about the underwater mountains gave him a precise indication of where and how far they were from the shore. He felt like some kind of sorcerer looking at a dome-sized map of the area, with the location of boats and land drawn on it.

"I don't even know which way is home," Kimi said, worry reflected in her eyes.

"It's ok," Ben reassured her. "I do."

He didn't tell her about the fuel, and she didn't ask, although he was sure the thought crossed her mind. He asked her to check around for anything useful.

Under a pile of wet towels, she uncovered two diving air tanks and two small bottles of water. She also found Jeremy's camera bag, which Ben had tossed into the dinghy before facing the SOVA captain. And from a pouch of the boat, she pulled out distress flares.

Kimi helped Jeremy drink from one water bottle and shared the second one with Ben. They gulped down thirstily.

Ben wondered whether he should tell Kimi about the plan that was forming in his head, but he knew she would object. So, he headed straight into the pitch darkness of night, away from land and followed the ocean current instead.

By the time the motor sputtered to a stop a couple of hours later, Ben knew he'd reached the place where he needed to be. Not only had he followed the ocean current for several miles to the approximate area of The Gathering, but from what he remembered during his previous connection with the blue whale, there were large container ships in the area.

The night had cleared up, revealing a half-moon that hung above the horizon.

Ben grabbed the flare gun, protected his face with his arm and fired at the sky. A bright, red glow arched into the night, waking Kimi with a start. She had fallen into a restless sleep some time ago.

"What's going on?" she exclaimed, searching the darkness for rescuers only Ben could see with his mind.

"It won't be long now," Ben said, half to himself.

"For what?"

The Gathering...

He took a deep breath. "We ran out of fuel," he told her. "But it's ok. There are ships in the area. They'll see the distress flare."

Kimi searched the darkness, then tensed. "Ben?" she said, turning to him with large eyes. "What are you talking about? There's nothing out there."

Ben forced a smile. "There is. More than you will ever know." He sucked in air and pointed to his left. "There are container ships there, there, and there. The second one is our best bet. That's the one I aimed for when I shot the distress flare. You'll need to repeat the shot every fifteen minutes."

"Me? What about you? And how would you know there are ships out there?" She stopped, eyes narrowing. "Wait a minute; you're up to something again, aren't you?"

Ben felt a shudder go down his spine, and he bit his lower lip to give himself courage. He turned so he wouldn't have to look at her and heaved one of the air tanks over his shoulders. "There's something I need to do…" he said before straightening and pointing at the lapping waves, "…down there."

She paled. "You're joking, right? Tell me you're joking."

Ben shook his head.

She flung the towel at him. "Why do you keep doing this?" she yelled. "I hate it when you do this! Did you even think to consult me? Do you think this is some kind of game? It's your life you're risking! Don't you think that matters?" Her nostrils flared. "Because it matters to me!" The words were barely out before she caught herself. She stepped back, visibly shaken, and plopped beside the outboard motor. "Please don't do it," she begged, and by the tone of her voice, Ben knew that she understood she had already lost the fight.

"I won't be long." He tried to sounds reassuring. "Keep sending the distress signal, then wait for me." He swallowed. "And if I'm not back by the time help arrives, call Mesmo."

Kimi pressed her lips into a thin line, crossed her arms over her chest and pretended to ignore him. She did not try to stop him when he sat at the edge of the dinghy but shot him a glare just before he let himself fall backwards into the sea.

Ouch!

His body hit the water, and he sank below the surface. The utter gloom turned his stomach to stone, and he almost gave up on his task right then and there. But something unexpected kept him going: Auntie Jen's warm face. Her words echoed in the darkness, *"Is there really such a place as The Edge of the Ocean, where half-moon and sea creatures meet? Perhaps we will never know. Or perhaps you are here to find out."*

And so, Ben dove deeper and deeper into the ocean realm.

It was so dark down there that he had to blink to make sure his eyes were open. It was one thing to experience the ocean world through the mind of a blue whale; it was a whole other thing as a human. The whale's senses gave him a perception that he did not have as a human. If he did not connect to a sea creature soon, his whole mission would fail. He scanned with his mind as far as he could, but not a single soul manifested itself to him. The underworld remained silent.

They don't want me!

The realization hit him. The blue whales had shut him out as soon as they had realized he was a human being.

They don't want me at The Gathering.

Ben tightened his fists, wondering what to do next.

And then it occurred to him that if they would not let him go to them, then he would have to make them come to him. It was time to test the limits of his skill. Would he be able to vocalize through the water the way the whales had?

He shut his eyes, willing the alien skill to wake within him. He searched for it within his heart, his blood, his soul. A tingling began at the tip of his fingers. He knew his hands glowed. There was no need to open his eyes to see. Electricity coursed through his body, his ears sang, and his brain burst with activity.

He remembered the blue whales' song as they had called the sea creatures across the ocean, and he repeated the notes, one after the other, louder and louder, over and over.

The reaction was immediate. In a heartbeat, the biggest blue whale connected with him from somewhere below him. His inner vision cleared, darkness evaporated, giving way to hidden valleys and mountains, forests of kelp, distant ships on the surface. A shoal of curious fish observe him from not too far.

But most of all, the biggest whale snapped him to attention.

How dare you! We told you to leave!

Ben stood his ground.

My name is Benjamin Archer, and you will listen to what I have to say.

He sensed the blue whales' anger as they emerged from the depths, their shadows growing larger and larger as they approached and surrounded him, for real this time. And it wasn't only the ten-story-tall mammals, but a myriad of other creatures, ranging from dolphins to sea turtles to bioluminescent phytoplankton. The tiny organisms flickered like millions of blue stars around him.

Something sharp brushed by him, tossing him into a spin, and black, gleamy eyes told him sharks lurked nearby.

The silence turned into a cacophony of hissing, bubbling and scratching voices. Unhappy, angry voices.

Get rid of the two-legged fiend!

Destroy him!

Others burst with alarm.

Hide!

It's a trap!

They will come for us!

Ben bellowed a single word. *SILENCE!*

The clamour died down at once. The gathered sea creatures considered him with a mixture of defiance and fear.

Ben toned down a notch. He could not afford to lose his audience.

I ask you to listen to me. Yes, I am a two-legged creature from the world beyond. Yes, I belong to a species that has continuously depleted and hunted you down. I understand your hate and fear of my kind, and it is well-founded.

Yet, I come here before you, defenceless, to offer you a truce. For I speak your language, and I also speak the language of my kind. Let me be the bridge between our worlds so you can transmit your injustices and requests, so our different species can come to an agreement, and balance can be restored.

Let me be a tool for you, so you no longer have to flee from us in fear, and your numbers no longer need to decline to a vulnerable level.

Silence fell over those gathered. The whales remained suspended around him in muted consideration. Sharks circled below his feet.

Ben insisted.

Let me help restore the natural balance that humans have broken. I can do that for you if you will let me.

One of the blue whales retaliated.

Why would you do anything for us? You are no better than the others of your kind.

A flutter of agreement reached Ben's mind.

Ben insisted: *Then do it for me. I am a child from the world beyond. I do not wish to live in a world where you no longer exist. You must take this step and connect with my kind, through me, so my children and my grandchildren may know you.*

A passing sea turtle slid by Ben's head and spoke with scorn. *Your kind will never listen to us.*

Ben tried to be conciliatory. *You are right: many will turn their backs or refuse to listen, but is it not our duty to try?*

One of the whales swung its tail in annoyance. *Enough!*

Craning his neck upward, Ben saw the outline of the whale's head, meaning dawn was approaching. Its voice was far from amicable.

We have let you speak, and now it is you who will listen. We have long considered disappearing to a place where your kind cannot find or reach us, and wait for the era of mankind to perish. Your offer is interesting. It is different, yet useless, nonetheless. You are but one child. What could one child do for the realm of the sea?

A new wave of agreement rotated around those present. Ben's stomach knotted. He was losing the debate, and losing was not an option. He clenched his jaw.

And you are but one whale! Yet you were a child, too, once. And here you are, today, leading The Gathering, surrounded by your followers. What would The Gathering be without you?

SLAM!

A shark knocked him so hard in the shoulder that his sight blurred. Angry shouts assailed his thoughts.

Ben grabbed his shoulder and blinked stinging tears from his eyes. The alien skill was to the point, all right, but jeepers! His diplomatic skills were in dire need of an upgrade.

He tried to come up with something smart to say, but it didn't help that his mask was askew, and his arm throbbed.

The sea creatures toyed with him, biding their time.

Waiting for a signal to attack!

The animals were becoming more defined. The sun would rise soon. There were so many of them closing in on him. He had to keep trying.

Why do you reject an opportunity to make things better? Why won't you let me transmit your plight to my kind? If humans heard your voice and understood you better, we could learn to live side-by-side. If you would only listen to the rest of my message...

It was useless. He sensed it as he probed the blue whale's mind from a safe distance. He hadn't made a single dent in their resolve. Humans were not worthy of sea creatures' attention. And Ben still belonged to humankind.

The whale confirmed his worst fear.

The Gathering has decided. You do not belong here. You and your kind have removed themselves from life's natural balance. You must now face the consequences, whatever they may be.

Life's natural balance: to eat or be eaten. Ben numbed. His voice sounded weak.

You are making a mistake.

The whales receded, making way for the sharks.

Ben turned, the predators circled him, closing in.

The first rays of sunlight pierced the ocean, and Ben wondered if Kimi was up there, somewhere, waiting for him. Would he make it to the surface in time, if he swam really hard? He didn't think so.

The bioluminescent phytoplankton faded away, and the blue whales broke the connection with him, leaving him in semi-darkness. The sharks circled like shadows on the edge of his mind.

I should have listened to Mesmo.

Had Mesmo not warned him about diving on his own? How strange, to be thinking about the alien man's disappointment while he was about to get ripped apart.

Then an unusual star descended towards him. Unusual, because it was red in colour. He had never seen a red star before. Another star appeared to his left, and another to his right, briefly startling the sharks away from him. Two of the red lights passed him by and continued into the depths. But the first one stopped by his face. The red flare was held by a hand that belonged to a person with a diving mask, topped with long, black hair.

Kimi!

She extended her hand to him.

Ben reached out.

An animal, much larger than the sharks, entered his field of vision, speeding towards them.

Kimi whirled towards the creature, making no attempt to escape.

Ben's eyes widened, a scream forming in his throat.

Too late!

The huge creature burst before them, stopping at the last second. *You will leave these children alone!*

Ben almost fainted. *Kana'kwa?*

The black and white orca spoke. *Yes, Benjamin Archer. I came as soon as I could. Are you all right?*

Ben's arms and legs weakened with relief. *I am now!*

Kana'kwa's pod arrived and circled them, while she remained close to the teenagers. She addressed the sea creatures, who observed the new developments from a safe distance. *Any creature intent on hurting these human children will have to go through me.*

The five whales sang in disapproval. *The Gathering has decided against them. Who are you to defy us?*

Kana'kwa insisted. *This child saved my pod and me. We would not be here were it not for him. Yes, humans caused our beaching, but it is also a human who saved us. The beings from the world beyond can be our downfall, but they can also be our lifeline. And I choose to pledge myself to them.*

The biggest whale bellowed. *You are too late, Kana'kwa. A consensus has been reached regarding this particular child. You will move aside or share his fate.*

CHAPTER 23 *The Message*

Jeremy woke to the sound of seagulls. The bright morning sunlight stabbed his eyes, and the swaying boat brought churning sensations to his stomach.

If only it would stop! That up and down motion of the boat. Up and down, up and down.

His insides heaved. He crawled to the side of the boat, leaning over to empty his stomach, only to find there was nothing left to expel.

"I hate boats!" he lamented to whoever would listen.

Except there was no one there.

He glanced around through cracked eyelids and stared at a seagull that landed on the outboard motor.

It squawked at him.

"What are you looking at?" Jeremy demanded. He stared at it with one arm hanging over the side of the dinghy, his hand dangling in the water, and racked his brain to figure out how he had gotten here. But his thoughts floated around like jelly.

The seagull squawked again.

"Yeah, yeah, I heard y..." Jeremy began, then gave up because the bird took flight. He stared after it, annoyed at having been ignored, then realized an impressive amount of birds were flying overhead. Didn't that mean there was land nearby?

He glanced over the side of the boat and froze.

The sea churned and bubbled like boiling water. Multiple shadows moved below the surface, bathed in bright blue light.

Why is there a blue light under the water?

He stared blankly at the phenomenon, figuring he must be experiencing a hallucination. He pinched himself, but the weird event continued.

A large fin broke the surface, making him yell. He pulled his hand out of the water and sprang to his feet, planting himself firmly in the middle of the dinghy.

Dolphin... It's just a dolphin!

His hands trembled with relief. Boy, was he glad it hadn't been anything more dangerous, because the mere act of standing had almost sent his stomach to his throat again.

Seagulls swept by his head, bypassing the churning blue water as if something had startled them. Jeremy turned and gawked.

There was something on the horizon. Something that was approaching. A wave? A storm?

He leapt to the outboard motor, feverishly trying to start it. But the engine spurted and went dead.

He blinked, searching in vain for something—*anything*—that would save him, then spotted something under a pile of towels. He reached for it and fished out his waterproof bag. Pulse quickening, he unzipped it and stared inside.

My camera!

Feeling like a toddler who had just found a long-lost toy, Jeremy took the camera lovingly out of the bag, held his breath and turned towards the mysterious tsunami that was heading his way. If these were going to be his last moments, he wouldn't go down without taking at least one picture.

* * *

Below the surface, Ben sensed the coming of new animals before he could see them. A clamour of voices reached his mind, and before he could react, an avalanche of creatures broke into The Gathering, swirling and dancing above, around and below them, causing havoc and confusion.

Kimi grabbed Ben's arm so hard he winced, pain shooting to his shoulder.

He watched in awe as diamond-shaped creatures dove between those gathered, splitting up groups and clearing the way for Ben and Kimi.

One of them stopped before the teens, and they stared at the giant manta ray that could have embraced them in its massive pectoral fins. This leader spoke with authority.

You will not touch these children. Not until you have heard what I have to say.

The swarm of manta ray that had just reached The Gathering slowed and hovered like flat spacecraft around the teens.

We have travelled a long way. We do not enjoy these cold waters. Yet it was necessary for us to come to The Gathering and confirm the orca's words.

A small manta ray, the size of a dinner plate, appeared next to the leader. It glided towards Ben and let him touch it. The leader continued:

This human child saved my grandson from certain death. Yes, my grandson was trapped in human garbage, yet it is also this human who saved him after our coral reef was destroyed. Only humans can undo the mistakes they have made. Do not be fooled. Hiding is not an option. Garbage will follow us to the depths of the ocean and suffocate us. Our survival depends on our capacity to face the humans from the world beyond, and this child can speak for us. Never before has a human spoken our language. This is our only opportunity. There will be no other. And so, for better or worse, we must accept his offer.

A lingering silence followed.

Ben forgot to breathe as The Gathering reconvened.

Then, out of the corner of his mind, he sensed the blue whales returning, the sharks moving away, the orcas and dolphins spreading out around him.

He glanced at Kimi and saw fear and wonder reflected in her eyes. He reached out his hand through the myriad of sparkling plankton and took hers, squeezing it in reassurance. Then they turned and faced the creatures of the ocean together.

Whalesong bounced through the water around them. *Speak, child. What is your message?*

In the midst of The Gathering, the alien skill alive and throbbing in his very core, Ben spoke to the sea creatures:

Listen, all of you! The time for the greatest gathering on Earth has come. A gathering that will be heralded for generations to come.

On the day of the winter solstice, when the sun is at its highest on the Equator, you will come to the mouth of the world's biggest river. You will send your leaders and your elders. You will spread the word far and wide among anything that crawls, swims, or flies that the time for humans and animals to unite has arrived. The time to mend life's broken balance has come. Spread the word that the time for The Great Gathering is here.

I will be there waiting for you. I will translate your burdens and your demands to the human leaders. I promise to be faithful to your words. You can count on me!

Ben fell silent and waited a moment that

lasted a lifetime. The sea creatures reconvened.

The blue whale spoke in acceptance: *We will spread the word, we will come and meet with humans.*

Voices echoed around those assembled. *We stand behind you, Benjamin Archer...*

CHAPTER 24 *Believing*

A container ship saved them by early afternoon. Right on time, too, because when Ben and Kimi resurfaced, they found a slightly delirious Jeremy waving his camera at them.

He said he'd never in his life seen, nor heard of such a frenzy of different animals gathered together in one place. And he had it all on film. This was going to be the article of a lifetime!

He clicked his camera at them, talking wildly, as whales breached, took a deep breath through their blowhole, then sank into the depths; orca headed towards the land, and manta ray disappeared into the horizon.

The pale reporter babbled on, even as they boarded the container ship, and the medically trained deck officer declared him incoherent due to extreme dehydration. No sooner had he checked Jeremy's vital signs, than the reporter passed out, flat.

Acting swiftly, Kimi picked up his waterproof bag and snuck it into Ben's hands.

Ben held on to it with a terribly guilty feeling in his stomach. *What should I do with the evidence?*

They were transferred to a smaller Coast Guard boat that dropped them off in Tofino, where a crowd of curious onlookers, worried locals, and reporters waited for them.

Ben could picture tomorrow's headlines: "Miraculous return of children lost at sea." "Teens safe after boat drifts away."

As they disembarked, the Coast Guard did their best to fend off the eager crowd who surrounded and bumped into the teens. A flurry of camera flashes and microphone wielding reporters overwhelmed them.

Ben thrust his arm before his face as if that would somehow protect his identity. He felt Kimi wrap her hand around his, and he clung to her like a lifeline.

"Dierenfluisteraar," a voice spoke sharply, just as Ben slammed into a row of men because the

crowd was pushing him.

A four-masted ship tattoo flashed before his face, and suddenly Wilson stood by his side.

Ben blinked, recognizing the row of men as Uncle Pete and police officers from the beach. They had slid into place before him and Kimi to form a protective barrier so the teens could slip away.

"Follow me," Wilson urged. "Let's get you out of here."

Ben hunched behind the men and followed Wilson, who jumped off the pier and dashed under it. It was low tide, so they were able to weave their way among the barnacle-encrusted rocks undetected.

Wilson reached a large boulder, which he clambered up with ease.

But as Ben watched Wil reach for Kimi to help her up, he chose to hang back. He turned and stared at the crowds on the pier, spotting Jeremy being taken away on a stretcher to an ambulance. Just then, the reporter happened to glance his way.

Ben flinched involuntarily, a primitive impulse pushing him to hide. But then he shoved the waterproof bag behind him, stood straight, and stared back at the reporter.

"Ben, what are you doing?" Kimi urged. "Hurry up before they see us!"

Ben stalled, pensive.

"Ben?" Kimi repeated with a touch of alarm in her voice. "What are you doing?"

Ben took a couple of steps back and glanced up at her. "Nothing," he said, before accepting Wilson's hand so he could climb up the boulder and vanish into the empty streets with them.

* * *

Uncle Pete, Auntie Jen, Wilson and the Sheriff listened to Ben and Kimi recount their adventures well into the night. Ben had begged Kimi beforehand not to reveal the part about The Gathering, a subject which she did a great job avoiding. No one spoke or asked any questions until they were completely done. After the Sheriff had taken plenty of notes and the Maesschalcks seemed satisfied that Ben and Kimi were okay, they sent them off to bed.

Ben couldn't believe it. He thought he'd get a

cringing sermon for having put Kimi in danger then be whisked away for good, never to see her again.

Instead, everyone treated him like a porcelain doll, fretting over him, trying to make him comfortable, and casting him curious looks when they thought he wasn't looking.

Uncle Pete only said not to worry about anything; the Sheriff would make sure the teenager's names wouldn't appear in the papers. As for the SOVA, the Marine Police Department was on high alert but had not been able to trace it down yet.

The family left Kimi and Ben alone, for which Ben felt immensely grateful. He let himself relax because he was still trying to process everything that had happened. It seemed like weeks since he and Kimi had gone out to meet the SOVA, yet only three days had passed.

As Ben found himself nodding off to sleep on the couch two days later, his memories took him under the ocean for the hundredth time, where he relived that sense of freedom he wished he could enjoy on land. And he also relived that moment of pride which he knew he would carry with him forever, for he had finally delivered the message he and Mesmo had crafted together.

"Are you ok?" Kimi asked, pulling him out of his half-slumber. She sat at the edge of the couch. "Sorry, I didn't mean to wake you, but you were squirming a lot. And..." She held Wilson's phone in her hand, looking a bit crestfallen. "...it's your mom. She says you have to go home."

Ben sat up straight. He took the phone from her with an *Uh-oh, I'm in trouble*-look.

She gave him a thumbs up. "You've got this!" she mouthed.

Ben watched her leave before clearing his throat and saying, "Hi, Mom."

"Hi, honey. How's it going?"

"Fine," he managed, biting his lip hard.

I'm going to have to tell her.

She didn't know yet. Wilson's family had said they were counting on Ben and Kimi to make the right decision. Ben knew he was going to have to tell his mom and Mesmo everything. He just didn't feel emotionally stable enough to do it right now.

"I know you're having a ton of fun out there," Laura said. "But Mesmo insisted I call to see if you can come home as soon as possible. He says the Wise Ones want to meet you. Mesmo thinks you being there might change their minds."

A wave of warmth washed over Ben,

knowing that Mesmo was considering his help. His mood brightened. "Yes! Actually, I do have something that will change their minds! You can tell him that."

"You're always full of surprises," Laura praised. "Look, you'll have to come back the *normal* way. By ferry, I mean, so I guess I'll see you tomorrow. Will you look into it?"

Ben grinned. "Sure, Mom. I'll text you the ferry arrival time as soon as I have it." He was going to hang up when he added, "And Mom?"

"Yes?"

"Sorry for being such a pain. And thanks for sending me to Tofino."

He could hear the smile in her voice. "I hope you got to eat some marshmallows and tell ghost stories by the fire. I can't wait to hear all about it!"

Ben grimaced as they said their goodbyes.

Poor Mom. She's going to throw a fit when she finds out...

Wilson entered, startling him. "Are you done napping yet, sleepyhead? We could do with a hand outside."

Ben grinned and followed him to the yard, where he found that neighbours and friends had arrived to help Uncle Pete rebuild his workshed.

Kimi passed him a piece of lumber, which

he held in place so Wilson could hammer nails into it. Together, it took them the rest of the afternoon to lift the structure. When they were done, Uncle Pete placed an arm around Ben's shoulders and cast a satisfying look at the final product.

The group clapped and laughed, a laid-back feeling washing over them. Auntie Jen brought out refreshments and sandwiches for everyone.

"Uncle Pete?" Ben asked, sipping on his fresh-pressed juice.

"Mmm?"

"You knew about the SOVA, didn't you? You knew it was there for the orcas?"

Uncle Pete smacked his lips, holding his cup in one hand and resting the other on Ben's shoulder. "We've had our suspicions. We already knew the local orcas were disappearing at an alarming rate in recent years, and not only because of ships like the SOVA. The orcas face many challenges, such as maritime traffic, which disturbs them, or because their food source—the chinook fish—are endangered. It wasn't the first time we've caught the SOVA lurking along the shoreline. But without definite proof of their illegal doings, I'm afraid there hasn't been much we could do. Let's hope you scared them off for good!" He squeezed Ben's shoulder and went to talk to his wife.

Ben stared at his cup. The SOVA was still out there. And he had proof to incriminate it.

Jeremy's camera.

Only, revealing the truth about the SOVA would also reveal the existence of his skill. How was he going to get around that?

* * *

Ben dreaded saying goodbye.

Auntie Jen stopped him at the front door. She held the leather-bound book containing the *Moon and Orca* story in her hands. "I think you should have this," she said, giving it to him.

Ben was stunned. "Oh, no! No way. I can't take this."

She smiled. "Yes, you can. And you will. I insist."

Ben swallowed as she hugged him.

"Thank you," he said, full of emotion. He hugged her back, then whispered, "Auntie Jen? I found it! The Edge of the Ocean."

She pulled back with a proud smile on her face and nodded as if that didn't surprise her at all. "Next time, I will tell you a different story, yes?"

Ben grinned, an electrical current rushing down his back at the prospect.

Wilson and Kimi drove him to the bus stop, where satisfied tourists boarded the bus that would take them back to their routine lives.

Wilson shook Ben's hand. "I apologize for calling you Ben-friend," he said. "From now on, I will call you *Fluisteraar.*"

Ben smiled shily. "Honestly? I kind of got used to Ben-friend." He picked up his loaded backpack and added, "Thanks, Wil. For everything."

Wilson nodded, but Ben noticed his eyes dart away as if something had distracted him. "What do you think?" Wilson whispered, sounding nervous. "Should I ask her?"

"Huh?" Ben glanced around, then realized Anna was scooping ice cream at the ice cream parlour at the street corner. "Ask her what?"

"You know..." Wilson said nervously. "...to marry me..."

Ben was going to laugh, then realized Wilson was deadly serious. "Um... gosh, Wil, aren't you rushing things a bit? I mean, aren't you supposed to ask her parents first, and... and get a ring and... and..." He slumped, at a loss for words, then grinned. "Sorry, dude, but you're going to have to figure this one out on your own."

"You'll come to the wedding, right?" Wilson burst as if it was a done deal. "I mean..." he stuttered. "...if she says, 'Yes.'"

Ben chuckled. "You bet, Wil. I'll be there."

Wilson let out a huge breath, his eyes taking on a dreamy state.

Ben smiled. "Enough of this saying 'goodbye' thing. Better get on with it, the summer's not getting any longer, you know?" He tapped the young man encouragingly on the arm.

They shook hands again, then Wilson took off with a giddy look on his face.

Kimi stalled by the bus door, shoving a pebble with her foot.

"I wish we could have travelled back together," Ben said when she looked up at him.

"Yeah, me too. Thomas and my mom are picking me up here in a couple of days. Too bad you won't get to see them."

Ben looked at his hands. "We're going to have to tell our parents, you know?"

Kimi puffed her cheeks. "I know. But after we tell them, I don't think they'll ever let us go on a camping trip again."

Ben pursed his lips.

She stared at the ground again. "Look, I'm

sorry I got angry at you before, for not telling me anything. I shouldn't have pressured you."

"Don't be sorry. You had every right to ask. I'm still surprised you believe my story. I know I wouldn't."

Her large, black eyes rested on his. "It's not really about whether or not I believe your crazy story, Ben. You heard Auntie Jen's tale. You'd think it was pure fantasy, but the thing is, each story is based on something real, each story has an element of truth hiding behind it. And in this case, I've come to the conclusion that that element of truth is you."

Ben stared at her, stunned. He wasn't entirely sure what she meant, but he knew it was something profound.

The bus roared to life, indicating it was time to go.

"Just remember," she said. "You may have some kind of superpower, but that doesn't mean you have to face everything on your own. Your mission is everyone's mission. There are people out there who will want to help. And I'm one of them."

"Boarding time!" the bus driver yelled.

She reached out and kissed his cheek, then stepped away.

Ben clambered on to the bus, almost tripping over himself. He took his place in a seat by the window, wanting to kick himself for not having come up with something smart to say. The least he could have said was *thank you*, but somehow Kimi had left him paralyzed.

Call me, she mouthed at him as he waved goodbye. He gave her a thumbs-up, then watched her as the bus drove off. He was going to settle back when he caught sight of Wilson reaching the ice cream parlour and Anna greeting him by throwing herself into his arms.

That's when Ben realized what Kimi had really meant. It wasn't that she needed to decide whether or not she believed in his story. It was that she had decided she believed in *him.* And that, somehow, meant more to him than anything she could ever have said.

CHAPTER 25 *Taking a Stand*

Ben had barely stepped out of his mom's car after a long drive from the ferry when she urged him to meet Mesmo under the maple tree.

The sun beat down on the cornfields, and when he shielded his eyes as he walked along the beaten path, he found a man walking up to him. He stopped and did a double-take because it was High Inspector James Hao.

Although Ben knew his mother had regular contact with the government agent, he had, until now, avoided any direct encounter with the man who had taken Tike away from him. He knew it hadn't really been the Inspector's fault, and he had saved their lives more than once since then, but Ben couldn't help associating traumatic memories with the High Inspector.

They faced each other, Ben struggling with mixed emotions. Since he had seen Hao last, the Inspector's hair had been grey above the ears, but now it had spread to the rest of his head.

"Benjamin Archer," Hao said. "It seems I find you wherever something unusual happens."

Ben didn't know what to say to that.

His English Shepherd dog ran up the path to greet Hao, his former master, and Hao obliged by giving the dog a good rub. Hao then loosened the button of his suit jacket and sat on a boulder by the side of the path.

"I'm glad we have a chance to talk," Hao said. "I know this must be as awkward for you as it is for me. I never got a chance to really apologize for what happened on the Kananaskis Mountains. I still think about it often and wish things had gone differently."

Ben was going to say, "It wasn't your fault." But his mind whirled with painful memories.

Still stroking Buddy's head, Hao looked at him. "You have to understand, I have been trained all my life to protect innocent people, and when I am ordered to track down a criminal target, I excel at doing so. Unfortunately, in your case, I was after the wrong target..."

Ben's eyes stung. "Everything that happened, happened because of Bordock. He hurt a lot of people in a lot of different ways. I remind myself of that every day. I know you didn't mean to do what you did. But I guess I... I just need some time..."

Hao nodded. "I understand." He stood and glanced at Ben. "Will you believe me if I tell you I have your back? No one understands the situation better than you, your mom, Mesmo, and me. We have been in this from the start. I hope that, should you ever need it, you will come to me for help."

"Thank you," Ben said. "You saved my mom and Mesmo. I'll never forget that." He lowered his hand and let the dog lick it. "And thanks for giving me Buddy."

Hao smiled sadly. "He's much better off with you. I'm hardly ever home now. Governments are barely making heads or tails of the situation, and I need to keep them on the right track. As long as I'm considered *The Cosmic Fall* expert, you'll have a buffer from prying eyes. I'll make sure it stays that way so you can accomplish whatever it is you have to do."

He glanced in the direction of the maple tree. "Mesmo has explained your new mission to me. You can count on me to get as many heads of state as possible to attend the international conference to be held in Brasil on December 21st. I look forward to seeing you there."

The Great Gathering!

Ben brightened. "That's a deal," he said, extending his hand. Hao's usually stern facial traits softened, and he accepted the gesture.

The handshake between them was firm.

As Ben walked away, his spirit lifted as he realized that Kimi was right. He did not need to do this on his own. People were rallying to his cause. He just needed a way to reach them.

His upbeat thoughts were short-lived, however, because when he reached the edge of the cornfield, he found the seven Wise Ones sitting in a circle, glancing his way with less than friendly eyes.

Mesmo stood, his eyebrows drawn together as if warning Ben to brace himself.

Ben held his breath, hoping no one noticed his wobbly legs as he approached the silent group. He could sense the tenseness in the air. There was no room for a chat; he had just landed in the middle of a war of words.

He sat beside Mesmo, and the latter spoke, "These are unusual times, and unusual times call for unusual measures. That is why I am authorizing this boy to join our meeting at your request. His name is Benjamin Archer. As you already know, my daughter entrusted him with her translation skill with her last dying breath." He looked at them in turn and added. "I trust you understand the meaning of such a burden."

Ben swallowed, searching for sympathy, but found none.

"Benjamin," Mesmo said, unfurling a hand in the direction of the man who sat to his left.

The elderly man wore a colourful hat with ear flaps—something that struck Ben as familiar because Mesmo had worn something similar in the past.

"This is Amaru, from Bolivia," Mesmo introduced him.

Amaru nodded with his sun-beaten face. Did Ben catch a hint of kindness in his wrinkled eyes?

"Beside him is Yakut, from the polar regions of Canada."

Ben nodded at the short woman with long, black braids flowing from both sides of her neck to her waist. She had a straight nose, high cheekbones and slanted eyes. Two parallel lines tattooed on her creased skin went from her mouth to her chin. He suddenly wondered how many stories these Wise Ones could have told, had the circumstances been different.

"Wonomanga is from Australia."

Ben stared shyly at the round-faced man who did not move an inch. His dark face and eyes were topped by thick, curly hair and a dense, graying beard.

"Akeya is from Kenya," Mesmo continued.

The woman smiled at Ben, and he breathed a little easier. Her black skin was flawless. She was bald and wore large, round earrings that dropped to her shoulders. "Welcome, Benjamin Archer," she said, sending a rush of hope through his heart.

"Kahalu is from the South Pacific," Mesmo explained. "She provided us with the information we used to visit the coral reefs in Polynesia."

Ben nodded in understanding, though the woman's multiple-braided hair, heavy eyebrows and parallel lines tattooed on her front did not show any emotion.

The next man's scowl turned Ben's blood cold. He had a white beard, shoulder-length hair tied in a bun, with one braid to the left and right of his head.

"This is Einar, from Norway," Mesmo said with slight contempt in his voice. He pointed to the last man with a white goatee, sitting in a wheelchair to their right. "And this is Su Tai from Chi..."

"That's enough!" Einar burst. "You insult us. Thousands of years and countless generations of service to the Toreq, and for what? For a boy who knows nothing!"

"Watch your mouth, Einar," Mesmo retorted.

Einar stood to his full height, his eyes on fire. "I have remained silent. I have listened to your positions with respect. But this crosses the line. I will not be part of your side project, Observer." His eyes threw daggers Ben's way. "My task on this planet was defined eons ago by the Toreq Arch Council. My ancestors and I have been faithful to it ever since. I will not be waylaid by a Toreq who has lost sight of our purpose and a human boy who does not belong here."

"Einar!" Akeya spoke sharply. "Mesmo is not some random Toreq. The Arch Council placed their full trust in him. His word is our command."

Einar smirked as if he had been waiting for this comment. "An interesting point, wise Akeya. One that I intended to raise myself. You see, now that the Observer decided—of his own accord—to return to Earth *indefinitely*, do you truly believe he still has the full support of the Arch Council?"

Akeya fell silent, and they all stared at Mesmo.

Ben balled his fists without realizing it.

Einar's voice dropped low. "Are we—Wise Ones—not a council of our own? Do we not come together to vote on important matters in the absence of word from the Arch Council? And in the absence of word from the Arch Council regarding the Observer, should we not be the ones determining his fate? For the day the Observer decided to join with the humans, well, did he not turn his back on his own people?"

Akeya hissed, "You undermine the Observer's authority, Einar. Your suggestion borders on mutiny."

The air was so tense Ben could barely breathe.

Amaru stood with difficulty and addressed the Norseman. "Einar, please, sit with us." He invited the imposing man to join them. Einar glared at him, then did so.

Amaru spoke. "We are faced with difficult questions, which we have discussed at length. Yet decisions cannot be made while emotions are high. We are all pained at not having been able to travel to the Mother Planet." He stared pointedly at Einar as he said this. "But let us not forget who is to blame here. It was the heinous shapeshifter, Bordock, who destroyed our transport home, who killed Mesmo's daughter, and it was his actions that left this young boy with the burden of a prized Toreq skill. Now, those of us present are left to deal with the consequences." He turned to Mesmo. "Observer, I believe I speak for all of us when I say the loss of your daughter weighs heavy on our hearts, and the sacrifice you made by returning to Earth is not lost to us, either. Your decision will be a great blow to the Arch Council. And, of course, to your father." He let the last words hang.

Most of the Wise Ones dropped their heads at hearing this last comment, startling Ben. He frowned at Mesmo, but the alien remained impassive beside him.

Amaru took in a deep breath, and continued, "However, it pains me to say there is some truth in Einar's words. The task of the Wise Ones is clear: we serve the Toreq by thoroughly registering human activity and reporting to the visiting Observers every two hundred Earth years. When possible, the Observer provides us with safe passage back to the Mother Planet in thanks for our services. This mission must continue until the Arch Council decides otherwise. That is all."

"Never has there been mention of meddling with human affairs. Never has there been mention of revealing ourselves to human governments. It is not the task of the Wise Ones to influence humans, change the course of their destiny or determine their fate. That last part is the task of the Arch Council. That is how it has been and how it always will be. Until the end of our mission."

Ben sprang to his feet. "You can't mean that!" He spoke before he could stop himself.

"Ben," Mesmo warned. "Not now."

"Yes, now!" Ben retorted, facing the Wise Ones. "How can you just sit by and watch? You have it easy, don't you? You've got your safe ticket to another planet. Why would you care what happens to this one? And yet you hold all the information in your hands to make things better, to teach us how to change, but you choose to hold it back and watch. There are creatures on this planet who are screaming for help. *Our* help. If they die, it will be as much your fault as ours."

"Ben," Mesmo repeated, taking his arm.

"No, I'm not finished. Were the Toreq not like us, once? Are you seriously going to tell me that they have always been the perfect civilization? That they never did anything wrong? They must have made mistakes and learned. So why will you not give us this chance to do the same? Why will you not teach us, instead of sitting by and watching from the sidelines? Are you not human, yourselves?"

Several Wise Ones shifted and glanced at each other. Ben caught Amaru give Mesmo a discreet smile. It caught him off guard but stifled his anger. Feeling like he had put himself in the spotlight, his cheeks flushed, and he took his place beside Mesmo again.

It was Einar who now stood, tense veins pulsing in his neck. Mesmo sprang to his feet as well, taking place before Ben, as if he were in need of protection.

Both men faced each other at eye level.

It seemed to take all of Einar's willpower to remain calm. "A'hmun blood ran through Bordock's veins. He robbed a Toreq skill and used it for evil. Why would it be any different with this human boy? He knows nothing of the ways of the Toreq. He knows nothing of Toreq skills. You turned your back on your people, Observer, and returned for this boy. I truly hope, for your sake, that he is worth it."

Mesmo's voice spewed molten lava. "You will cease your threats, Einar, and discuss the matters at hand, or I will strip you of your title. I take it you would not want to be known as the one who put shame on your lineage?"

Einar's nose curled as if he did not like what he was hearing, but his steady gaze showed he was not afraid of Mesmo. He straightened and turned to the others. "And hence, I return to my original question: is the Observer still the Observer? Has he not turned his back on his kind? Has he not chosen Earth citizenship above his own? I call for a vote!"

Murmurs rippled around the circle.

Mesmo dropped beside Ben.

Akeya lifted her angry voice. "You would strip the Observer of his Toreq rights and remove him as head of our group?"

Einar sat with a smug look on his face without answering her.

"Can they do that?" Ben whispered.

Mesmo nodded. "If a vote is called, all members are required to participate."

Voices rose and ricocheted from one side to the other.

"Einar is protecting our position."

"But the boy is right; we are accessories to crimes of humanity."

"The Observer is stuck here, just like us."

"He rescinded his Toreq rights the day he

returned."

"But that's not fair!" Ben chimed in.

Mesmo raised his hands to silence the group. "Einar has called upon you to vote. What is your decision?"

Einar smirked. "Place yourself in the shoes of the Arch Council. Raise your hand, those in favour of stripping the Observer of his Toreq citizenship, meaning he will be banished from our circle and live among humans, never again to mention our existence." He lifted his hand high.

CHAPTER 26 *High Stakes*

Ben stared from one to the other in alarm. Were they really going to allow such a vote, after everything Mesmo had gone through?

Wonomanga and Kahalu hesitated, then raised their hand.

Einar's expression tightened as he waited for more votes. When no further hands raised, he fumed, "Do you not understand what you are voting for? If the Observer remains, he will ask you to reveal yourselves to the world, to share your knowledge and teach humans the ways of the Toreq. You will directly influence their development, meaning you will defy a direct order from the Arch Council. Are you willing to take that risk?" His eyes fell on Amaru. "Amaru, did you not say you agreed with me?"

The Bolivian man did not seem fazed by the Norseman's digs. "I may not agree with the Observer, Einar. But until the Toreq Arch Council replaces him or reverts its support of him, it is crystal clear to me that Mesmo *is* the Arch Council, here on Earth."

Einar's face reddened. "Fool! It will take two hundred years before we hear from the Arch Council again. Mesmo will long be dead by then. And as you all know, the Toreq way forbids him to take on another spouse or bear children." His eyes darted accusingly Mesmo's way, and Ben felt the alien tense like an arrow. "Who knows who he would leave in his place?" Then, his eyes shifted to Ben, and he paled as if he had just found the answer to his question.

Mesmo said in his most neutral voice, "The vote stands three against four. Your request is denied, Einar."

The Norseman's eyes narrowed. "That's one vote short, Observer. You may not be so lucky next time." He stood and straightened.

"This meeting isn't finished," Mesmo growled.

"It is for me," Einar seethed. And with that, he turned and left.

It wasn't long before Kahalu rose, gazed at Mesmo, then walked away without a word.

Wonomanga stood as well. "Forgive me, Observer," he said. "But voting otherwise would go against my conscience. I cannot change my ways; it has been too long."

Mesmo nodded once. "I understand, Wonomanga."

The old man took his walking stick and headed away.

Those who remained cast each other sidelong glances, until Mesmo spoke. "Thank you for your vote of confidence, my friends. Contrary to Einar's opinion, voting for me does not mean you are voting for my new mission."

He gestured towards Ben. "Benjamin and I are not bound by the same promise your ancestors made to the Arch Council tens of thousands of years ago. The boy has decided that he must use his skill to help humans and creatures of this planet live in balance with each other. It is a bold decision for such a young one, and he will need all the help he can get.

"I, for one, stand by him. Not only because he holds my daughter's legacy, but because I know him, and he is deserving of my full support. For is he not the type of human that the Toreq would wish to see more of? The type that the Toreq could negotiate peace with? So, I ask, but do not command, that you help him in any way you can. You are already aware that The Great Gathering will take place..."

"...at the mouth where the greatest river meets the ocean," Ben breathed.

"Brazil, at the mouth of the Amazon River." Mesmo nodded. He paused, then said, "I can't force you to follow us down this same path. However, it would be unfair to place the whole burden on this young child's shoulders. I have pledged to help him in any way I can, and I hope you will, too."

Akeya smiled. "I stand by you all the way, young Benjamin. And you, Observer, you can count on me. I will head home at once and begin sharing my knowledge with all who will listen."

"I will do what I can, Observer," Su Tai said. "Though I am old and on my way to retirement. I must speak to my daughter about her new responsibilities, so she may carry forth this new flame you give us."

Yakut, the woman from polar Canada, remained silent, but when she spoke, her words were parsed and studied. "I applaud your efforts, you and the young one's. I will share my knowledge with my human kin, though I strongly suspect they will not listen." She paused. "My only fear is that it is too late, and I regret the Arch Council did not order this done many generations ago."

"I agree," Amaru said. "The Great War of the Kins is long behind us. The Arch Council should have given the descendants of the A'hmun a second chance a long time ago. It is because of this lack of openness that crooked elements like Bordock have surfaced."

Mesmo spoke, "Bordock said he wanted humans to survive so that one day they could take their rightful place on the Mother Planet. Meaning he would see the Toreq decimated and replaced by humans."

Akeya gasped. "If Einar hears of this..." she let the sentence hang.

Mesmo nodded. "Indeed, if Einar hears of this, nothing will change his mind to help us. But what worries me more is that Bordock did not act on his own. He was sent here."

"By whom?" Su Tai exclaimed.

Mesmo looked at them in turn, then sighed and said, "That is something we may never know. It will take us two hundred years to find out what is happening on the Mother Planet. I pray the warning I sent the Arch Council through the wormhole will help them uncover the treacherous elements who sent Bordock. If they don't act on this, an underground movement of hidden A'hmun could grow and become a danger to the Toreq."

Yakut gasped, "I understand now, why you wish to help humans. Should this rogue A'hmun faction truly exist on Torequ'ai, we will want humans on our side to face this new threat."

Ben stared at Mesmo with wide eyes.

"You read me well, Yakut," Mesmo said. "I can see only gain from helping Earth humans. We restore the broken balance between Earth's inhabitants, we help them reach a healthier civilization that will align with the Toreq's, we negotiate peace between our peoples, and then the rogue A'hmun faction will have no reason for being."

"Are you not overly ambitious, Observer?" Su Tai said softly.

Mesmo grimaced. "Probably. But I can't sit around and watch humans destroy their habitat, just as I can't watch Bordock's masters grow stronger on the Mother Planet."

They fell silent.

Ben beamed at Mesmo.

Then Akeya said, "Your father would be proud of you, Observer."

CHAPTER 27 *Unidentified Flying Object*

Mesmo watched Su Tai, Yakut, and Akeya disappear down the path through the cornfields. Only Amaru and Ben remained behind.

Ben sagged onto his back, puffing through his cheeks. "Oh, man! That was intense!"

Mesmo turned and stood over him. "You, my friend, are grounded."

"Huh?" Ben squinted up at him. "What did you just say?"

"I said, you're grounded," Mesmo repeated, then added as an afterthought. "For the rest of the summer."

"You... I'm... *whaaat?*" Ben pushed himself up to rest on his elbows. "Now, where did you learn a word like that?"

Mesmo rubbed his chin. "I don't know. Must be your mom. Or a TV show."

Ben gave him a scornful look. "Seriously? I think you watch way too much TV..."

Mesmo shut his eyes and shook his head. "Don't change the subject! I told you not to get into trouble!"

"I... what? What trouble? I..." Ben stood in haste, brushing away the dust from his trousers. He blinked rapidly, then his shoulders drooped. "How... um... who told you?"

"I read it in the paper. A reporter from the Provincial Times was found drifting out on the ocean, after trying to cover the event of the beached orcas. He said that two teenagers were with him, but their names were not released because they were under-aged." Mesmo's eyes narrowed. "Your mom didn't see it. And I haven't told her yet."

Ben fumbled, glancing around as if searching for help. "I... I was going to tell you about it, I swear! It's just, I've been so busy, and you were in the meeting and... and..." He waved his hands around helplessly, then groaned. "Ooh! I forgot! Mesmo, I connected with the ocean creatures. They have accepted our message. They will spread the word and come to The Great Gathering on the day of the winter solstice."

"That's enough, Benjamin. You have some explaining to do. I want you to go home and talk to your mother now. I will join you in a minute."

"But..."

"I said, *now!*"

"Ok, ok. Back off already. I'm going!" Ben shot him a stupefied look. "Er... Goodbye, Amaru," he said, stumbling a little as he shook the Bolivian man's hand.

"*Adios*[7], Benjamin," Amaru smiled.

Ben headed off towards the fringe of cornfields. "See? I'm going already," he yelled without turning around.

Mesmo grinned. "Benjamin?" he called.

"What?"

Mesmo waited for Ben to glance over his shoulder. "I'm proud of you."

Ben rolled his eyes. "Yeah, yeah, whatever," he yelled back, but Mesmo caught the smile that spread on the boy's face just before he turned to walk away.

Mesmo and Amaru watched him until he disappeared from view, insect sounds taking over

---

[7] Adios = Spanish word meaning "Goodbye".

the silence. Even then, they waited several minutes more, until Amaru figured it was safe to speak. "Einar has taken a dislike to the boy," he said.

"Einar dislikes many, Amaru," Mesmo pointed out, then pursed his lips. "Though I wish I hadn't had to involve Benjamin in this."

"I don't agree. Everything went as planned. By involving the High Inspector, and then the boy, you forced Einar to make a move, which, in turn, forced the others to take a position."

"Clever, that," Mesmo complimented Amaru. "To make Einar believe you were going to vote in his favour."

"He will not forgive me that easily. And he will not forgive you, either, which brings me to the next point. All Einar needs is to sway a single vote his way to be rid of you. And that leads me to another worrisome thought."

Mesmo grimaced. "I'm sure you're going to tell me."

Amaru stared at Mesmo. "You do realize, of course, that once you are out of the way, the boy will no longer fall under your protection in the eyes of the Wise Ones?"

Mesmo placed a hand on Amaru's shoulder. "Then, let's make sure it doesn't get to that. Let's not lose sight of our goal. A great milestone has been achieved. The High Inspector is our trusted link to human leaders; Benjamin is our link to the animal kingdom; and I am the link to you, Wise Ones. Together, we can move mountains. Let us make sure The Great Gathering is successful."

"*Muy bien*[8]," Amaru said. "Then, that leads me to one last thing."

"I can't wait," Mesmo grimaced.

Amaru glanced at the large shed at the back of the house. "We have to talk about your spaceship," he said.

Mesmo frowned, following Amaru's gaze. "My spaceship? Ah, yes, I know the shed is not the best hiding place. I haven't gotten around to finding a better spot yet..." He trailed off because Amaru bent to pick up a bag made of colourful cotton ropes with a rough llama design on it.

The Bolivian man pulled out an iPad, which he activated. "Mesmo, *amigo*[9], I strongly recommend you start using human means of transportation. Or, at least, you could be more discreet when you use your spaceship."

---

[8] Muy bien = Spanish for "Very well".

[9] Amigo = Spanish for "Friend".

"What are you talking about?" Mesmo asked, leaning over to watch a video that Amaru selected.

Undeniable proof aliens are here, the title read. *The ten best UFO videos. Watch before they get removed!*

Mesmo shook his head in disapproval. "Amaru, don't tell me you watch these things. You know they're all fake, don't you?"

Amaru gave him a sideways glance. "Not this one," he said, selecting one of the videos.

A grainy image showed the roofs of a heat-stroked city on a yellow afternoon. The person shooting the video gasped into the camera and zoomed towards distant mountains, lost in hazy heat. A black spot sped before the camera, then came to a sudden full stop. The cameraman commented excitedly, clearly mentioning the unidentified object.

Suddenly the UFO shot up into the sky in a flash of light and disappeared into a lone cloud, which followed it with wisps of air. The video replayed in slow motion with a much stronger zoom.

Mesmo gasped. "But that's my spaceship!"

"Yes, amigo. You need to be more careful about how you fly it in the future, especially with so many smartphone-obsessed people out there."

Mesmo leaned closer. "Wait a minute," he said. "It says '*Stunning video footage of UFO over rural Istanbul, as seen yesterday.*'" Mesmo straightened. "I never flew over Istanbul, Amaru. I was here with you all day yesterday, remember?"

Amaru stared at the video, as if, by doing so, it would somehow make sense. He turned to Mesmo with troubled eyes. "But, Mesmo, if that wasn't you, then who was it?"

EPILOGUE

Jeremy Michaels placed his elbows on his office table and leaned his forehead in the palm of his hands. As soon as he closed his tired eyes, memories flashed before his eyelids: the SOVA, fighting off rogue sailors, the two kids, falling into the freezing water and then...

And then... what?

He pressed harder with his hands.

Feeling horribly, horribly sick, sea creatures everywhere, weird lights in the water...

That last part couldn't be right, of course. He must have hallucinated. That's what the deck officer on the container ship had said. Jeremy just wished he could distinguish fact from fiction. He knew his severe dehydration had affected his memory, but he also had a keen intuition, and that intuition told him major things had happened. His notebook full of questions made this painfully evident.

Questions are good, he reminded himself. Questions helped reporters discover what needed to be put in the spotlight.

He opened his eyes and glanced at the pile of research papers he had pulled up about beached whales, factory ships, governments allowing the plunder of the ocean... He could have written a major piece, one that would have been picked up by the media worldwide. But it was all in his head, and he didn't have a shred of proof.

Feeling miserable, Jeremy pulled up a search engine on his computer screen and slowly typed a name with his index finger, pressing one key at a time in a bored manner: S-O-V-A. Then he pressed ENTER. The search results appeared.

SOVA: Russian word meaning 'owl'.

Jeremy sighed.

Well, that's just great. Not helpful at all.

Had he really expected a picture of the grim ship to magically appear on the screen? He hadn't found a trace of the ship in any maritime listings and, anyway, the crew could have painted over the name plenty of times by now.

With an angry swipe of his arm, he shoved the pile of documents into his trash bin and stared at it as if it were going to solve all his problems.

"Hiya, rookie. I didn't think you'd still be here." His colleague peered over the office space panel. He rested his arm on its edge and smiled smugly at the reporter.

Jeremy scowled. The guy wasn't referring to working late at the office; he was referring to the fact Jeremy hadn't been fired.

"'Course I am," he mumbled, fighting to make his voice sound matter-of-fact. "Why wouldn't I be?"

His colleague shrugged as he pushed his glasses further up his nose. "Oh, it's just something I heard about the boss being livid because he sent you to cover a surfing heaven, and instead, you somehow managed to lose your professional competence in the middle of the Pacific Ocean."

Jeremy focused hard on his screen, boiling inside. "Are you done already?" he seethed.

"Not quite. Does he know you also *misplaced* your camera?"

Jeremy's eyes sent invisible lightning bolts at his computer.

His colleague chuckled. "Didn't think so. Good thing it's your lucky day." He reached over the panel and plonked a very smelly waterproof bag on the desk.

Jeremy's eyes popped out of his head.

His colleague clicked his tongue. "You can thank me later," he said as he turned to leave.

"Huh? W-Wait. W-What?" Jeremy couldn't stop gaping at the bag. He blinked, willing the wheels in his brain back into action, then ripped the zipper open. His camera and a very smelly wrapped piece of fish lay inside. "Hey! Wait a second!" He leapt out of his chair and glanced over the panel.

His colleague was already halfway across the spacious office room, strolling with one hand in the pocket of his classy suit pants.

Jeremy grabbed the camera, incredulous to be holding his favourite object, and rushed after him. "Wait a minute. How did you get this?"

The guy straightened his glasses and shrugged. "Dunno. Ask the receptionist. She..."

Jeremy didn't listen. He left his colleague stranded with his mouth open in mid-sentence and weaved through the employees who were leaving for the day.

The blonde receptionist lifted her head as he charged towards her.

"Where did you...?" he started, then heard one of the elevators ping. The doors began to close on a crammed lift, with Ben Archer staring in his direction.

"Hey, you!" Jeremy shouted, sprinting across the hall. "Hold it!"

Too late! The doors shut just as he slammed against them. The elevator call button refused to respond.

Jeremy spun around and headed towards the emergency stairs, flying down them two steps at a time. He burst into the main hallway, but the elevator had already emptied, its last occupants zigzagging around each other in their haste to get home. Jeremy stretched his neck in search of the kid, then, not finding him, rushed outside and scanned the busy street. A person with a grey hoodie slipped into a service street.

Gotcha!

Jeremy followed close on his heels. He turned a corner, then skidded to a stop.

Ben Archer stood waiting for him, his hands in the pockets of his hoodie sweatshirt, his side fringe covering part of his left eye.

All senses alert, Jeremy approached the kid slowly, looking left and right, half expecting to be ambushed by the ship-tattoo guy.

"It's just me," the kid said. "No-one knows I'm here." He wouldn't meet Jeremy's eyes. The kid cleared his throat. "I slipped out of the house. I'm supposed to be grounded."

"Is that so?" Jeremy asked, lifting an eyebrow. He lifted his camera and waved it in Ben's face. "And this?" he demanded.

"It's your camera. I thought you'd want it back."

"Did you now?" Jeremy snapped, taking a good look at the object for the first time.

"You'll find it intact."

Jeremy grimaced. "Intact, huh? Does that count for its contents, too?" *Kid must've wiped out all my pictures!*

As if reading his mind, Ben said, "It's all there." He gestured at the camera. "Everything."

The way the kid stressed the last word, startled Jeremy. He stuck his tongue in his cheek and sized up the boy, trying to decide whether to hug him or scold him. "Tell me. What am I going to find? I need to know."

"I'm sure you remember."

Jeremy hesitated. *Lights in the water, a swarm of sea creatures...* "I saw... things... under the water. I need to know. Was I hallucinating?" Stomach twisting, he hissed, "And don't play games with me."

The kid held his breath as if he were about to plunge into the deep end of a pool. Then, he said, "No, Jeremy. You weren't hallucinating. It was all real."

Jeremy lowered his hand that held the camera. There wasn't an inkling of mischief in the kid's eyes.

Ben took another deep breath and said, "I need your help. I need you to write an article, about the beached orcas, about the SOVA, about the packaged fish we found in the ship's hull, how you saved us and how we escaped and... about the rest."

"The rest?"

The kid nodded. "Yes. I need governments to take action on ships like the SOVA. They mustn't be allowed to operate; overfishing needs to end. The local orca population needs to be restored. The subjects you could write about based on your pictures are endless."

While the kid spoke, Jeremy had turned on his camera and swiped through the most recent pictures. Goosebumps rose on his arms. He felt like he was hallucinating all over again. There they were: the hundreds of manta rays jumping out of the sea, massive whale snouts surging from the surface, glimmers of bioluminescent krill visible on the waves in the dawn light, an orca pod basking calmly near the boat and, in the midst of it all, the boy. Jeremy raised his head and stared at him.

Ben said, "I came to say I'm sorry for taking your smartphone and for keeping your camera. It wasn't right. And I wanted to thank you for saving Kimi and me. Who knows where we'd be if it weren't for you."

Jeremy's mind whirled. "But why? Why didn't you come forward before? Why did you keep the camera?"

The kid bit his bottom lip, sizing him up, then said, "Because there's something else I need to tell you."

Jeremy raised an eyebrow. "What's that?"

Full-fledged resolve shone in the boy's eyes. "I need to tell you about my skill."

THE ADVENTURE CONTINUES:

Ben Archer and the Star Rider

www.amazon.com/dp/B086RK31LT

LEAVE A REVIEW:

If you enjoyed this book, please leave a review in the 'Write a customer review' section:

www.amazon.com/dp/1989605044

PREQUEL:

Read the prequel to The Alien Skill Series,

The Great War of the Kins:

www.raeknightly.com

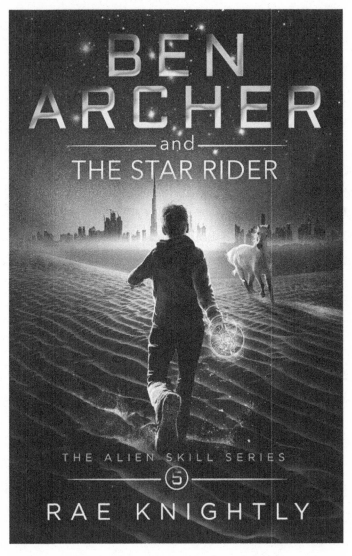

BEN ARCHER
and
THE STAR RIDER

THE ALIEN SKILL SERIES
5

RAE KNIGHTLY

Turn the page and start reading...

CHAPTER 1 *The Animal Whisperer*

The half-open briefcase revealed row upon row of neatly stacked dollar bills, ready for use.

The man in the white leather chair did not seem very interested in it, however, as he did not take his eyes off the large television screen on a TV stand. Beside it, an office desk held two computers.

The man pressed the buttons on his handheld gaming control, watching intently as his avatar got slammed from all sides by the enemy. His concentration did not waver, even when a servant slipped into the room and stood by his side.

The servant with a clipped, dark-brown beard whispered something in the man's ear.

The man's fingers froze on the control, his avatar getting trampled under the words: **GAME OVER**

The man leaned back into his chair, deep in thought. He then picked up a different control and pressed the replay button.

"Thank you! Thank you!" A woman filled the screen and grinned at the audience, before sitting in a plush sofa on the set of a television program called *Charlie's Chit-Chat Show*, the name of which was sprawled on a glittery backdrop behind her.

"I'm so glad you're here to welcome our special guest tonight. He's a young boy who comes to us from Canada and who made headlines recently when he was photographed in a rather unusual setting. But let's ask him to tell us his story. Please welcome Benjamin Archer!"

Loud applause followed as a boy entered the scene and sat opposite the blond host. His brown eyes matched his brown hair, which was neatly combed to the side, though, unfortunately, the show's make-up artist had missed a rebellious mesh that stuck out from the back of his head. He wore jeans and a navy-blue collared shirt under a dark grey hoodie sweater that was unzipped at the front.

The show host crossed her slim legs and said, "Hello, Benjamin. Thank you so much for coming out here from your native town of Chilliwack, located on the West Coast of Canada."

The boy cleared his throat. "Um, thank you. And, um, people just call me Ben."

"Right you are, Ben. Now many of us have seen the stunning pictures which were taken by the famous reporter Jeremy Michaels. For those who don't know what I'm talking about, let's take a look..."

The glittery screen disappeared behind her and turned into an image of the ocean, the waters of which were crawling with the most unusual gathering of sea creatures, ranging from whales to orcas, to manta rays. Several similar images scrolled before the audience, who let out exclamations of wonder, not only because they were so spectacular, but also because, in the midst of each one, Ben Archer's head bobbed in the water.

"Isn't that amazing?" Charlie gasped. "Benjamin... Ben. I think I voice everyone's question when I say: what on Earth are you doing in those pictures?"

A ripple of laughter came from the audience.

"Um... it's a gathering of animals that live in the ocean. They come together like this, once or twice a year, but it had never been recorded before."

"But you're in the middle of it all! Weren't you terrified?"

"I was, at first, until I understood what the animals wanted of me."

Charlie let out a little chuckle. "Hm, yes. These images are astounding in themselves, but it seems there's more to it than that. You claim that you can actually *talk* to these animals. Some people are even calling you an 'animal whisperer'. Why don't you tell us about that?"

The boy shuffled in his seat, then said in a clear voice, "An animal whisperer? Yeah, I guess you could say that. It happened about a year ago. I started hearing my dog's thoughts..."—his voice faltered briefly while the audience chuckled— "then other animals started talking to me, like crows, whales, bees... They were all telling me the same thing. They are sick. And we're making them sick. It's not just that we're destroying their habitat and causing their numbers to dwindle, it's that more and more are showing signs of illness that will spread like wildfire if we don't do something soo..."

"Wait a minute, wait a minute!" Charlie interrupted. "Go back a bit. You said, 'other animals began talking to me'. Do you realize what you are saying?"

The audience laughed a little too hard.

The boy blinked at her, a touch of annoyance showing in his face. "Yes, that's what I said. Animals speak to me, and I can speak to them. I have offered myself as a translator to the animals, and they have accepted."

The host waved her hands at him as if he were going way off track. "Ben, Ben, hold on a minute. You do understand that claiming to be an animal whisperer is a little hard to swallow for us normal folks here. Tell me, how old are you?"

"Thirteen. Almost fourteen," the boy said with a touch of defiance in his voice. "But this isn't about my skill; this is about what we're doing to our planet..."

"Wait! Before you say anything else, you will agree that we need some kind of proof of this superpower of yours. It's one thing to see these incredible pictures, but I thought we could do a little test, right here, in the studio. What do you think?"

The crowd whistled and cheered.

The boy tensed. "What kind of test?"

Charlie laughed. "Oh, nothing serious, I promise."

As she spoke, a spotlight came on to illuminate another part of the stage, which was separated by a curtain that dropped down from the studio ceiling so the host and guest couldn't see what was happening behind it. Only the audience could. A man rolled in a small, wheeled table with a cage on it. A furry white rabbit stared out its bars.

"Oooh!" the audience cooed.

Charlie grinned. "Ben, we have a real, live animal behind that curtain..."

"You mean the rabbit?" Ben interrupted, his face slightly flushed.

"Wow!" the audience laughed, with sporadic clapping as some hadn't quite caught what had just happened.

"Yes, well done!" She turned to the audience and said, "I promise, this is all happening live. Ben didn't know about this."

Excitement built up as another animal was brought on stage.

Charlie waved her hand at the crowd. "Don't say anything! Let's give Ben a chance."

Clearly, the boy was no longer enjoying the show, but he had no choice but to go along with it. He guessed the next animals: a tortoise, a goldfish and a snake.

The audience buzzed while Charlie giggled. "How fun!"

"Yes," the boy said without conviction. "And now I need to tell you how we are endangering the very lives of..."

"Oh, wait a second, Ben. We only have a few more minutes. This is the last one."

Cheering erupted from the audience as a beautiful, brown horse was brought on stage. Its ears flicked back and forth on its head.

"Come on, Ben, we're counting on you," Charlie beamed as if she could see the number of viewers of her show rising off the charts.

This time the boy stood, a look of worry on his face. "You should get that horse off the stage," he said.

Loud applause.

The horse pawed at the ground and pulled at its bridle, giving its handler a hard time as he tried to keep it in tow.

Charlie clapped her hands in delight.

"No, really," Ben warned. "The horse is scared. She can smell the presence of the snake."

He had barely spoken when the horse reared, knocking over its handler. It then crashed through the curtain into the glaring spotlights, neighing in fear.

Charlie shrieked and fell off her sofa.

Ben jumped in front of her, placing himself between the host and the terrified horse. Lifting his hands high, he stood his ground before the animal, which shook its mane to-and-fro and snorted loudly.

The boy didn't move an inch, while Charlie held her hand to her heart, mouth agape and eyes wide.

The brown mare pawed at the ground, its skin gleaming in sweat as it snuffed through its nostrils.

The audience watched, aghast, as the boy presented his hands to the horse, palms outstretched. The animal backed away, body trembling, ears down. Then it seemed to change its mind. It approached the boy slowly, gave a kind of bow and rested its snout in the boy's hand until it became fully reassured.

The boy's tense body relaxed. He reached out to rub its neck...

The man in the white leather chair pressed the pause button, freezing the screen on the boy and the horse. He rubbed his chin for a moment, then glanced at the money-filled briefcase. With the smallest gesture of his hand, the servant sprang into action, locking its lid and hurrying down the hall to a back entrance.

Two heavy-set men in business suits stood waiting in the glaring sunlight.

The servant handed the briefcase to one of them and said in broken English, "You get other half after it is done."

The one holding the briefcase glanced at the other through black sunglasses.

"You have Master's instructions," the servant insisted. "He wants the boy."

Continue reading:
Ben Archer and the Star Rider
(The Alien Skill Series, Book 5)
www.amazon.com/dp/B086RK31LT

About the Author

Rae Knightly invites the young reader on a journey into the imagination, where science fiction and fantasy blend into the real world. Young heroes are taken on gripping adventures full of discovery and story twists.

Rae Knightly lives in Vancouver with her husband and two children. The breathtaking landscapes of British Columbia have inspired her to write The Alien Skill Series.

Follow Rae Knightly on social media:
Facebook/Instagram/Twitter/Pinterest
E-mail: raeknightly@gmail.com

Acknowledgments

To Ricardo, whose spirit lives on in his model boats.

To Whales and Dolphin Conservation (WDC) for their input on the Pacific Coast killer whale population.

To Bob Bush, Robin Campbell, Giselle Schneider, R. Mark Jones, Ian Ness, D'artagnan Maciel, Paul Hill, Frank Muellersman for catching the literary bugs hiding under the rug. Special thanks to Mystee Pulcine and Cristy W.

To you, reader, for taking the time to read *Ben Archer and the World Beyond*.

Thank you!
Rae Knightly